THE UNSUITABLE DUKE

LANDING A LORD

SUZANNA MEDEIROS

To Emma and Faith. Because dreams do come true.

THE UNSUITABLE DUKE

An enemies-to-lovers romance.

When they were children, Ellen Laughton considered the Duke of Castlefield her best friend. But when he learned their parents were hoping they'd marry one day, he did what any boy of twelve would do—he pushed her away.

She's been angry with him ever since.

By the time Castlefield realized there was only one woman for him, Ellen was already betrothed to another. Now that she's a widow and out of mourning, he is determined to win back her friendship and her heart.

But when Ellen learns about the role he played in her husband's death, will she be able to forgive Castlefield's betrayal?

To learn about Suzanna Medeiros's future books, you can sign up for her new release newsletter at: https://www.suzannamedeiros.com/newsletter

CHAPTER 1

July 1807

HE DUKE OF CASTLEFIELD scanned the glittering crowd from his position by the ornate garden doors. She was here, deuce take it. He could feel it in his bones.

For what felt like the hundredth time, his eyes swept over the women currently partnered on the ballroom floor before he started skimming over the guests gathered along the outer edges of the brightly lit room. But the stubborn bane of his existence remained hidden. The fact that everyone wore masks to conceal their identity wasn't the impediment. He'd know Ellen anywhere. Which meant she was biding her time before making her presence known.

If he remained patient, she'd eventually reveal herself. She wouldn't be able to resist the desire to harass him. He was counting on that now as he slipped through the open doors that led out to the gardens. He made his way to the far side of the balcony and turned to look out into the darkness. He wasn't the only person outside that evening, but he was the only one who hadn't sought a darkened corner for his meeting. He stood alone, light from the ballroom spilling out onto the balcony and making his figure visible. He did want to be found after all.

He didn't have to wait long before he sensed movement to his left. Still, he continued to stare out at the lush greenery before him, his every instinct on high alert as she moved closer.

I have you now, he thought, resisting the urge to smile. "I was wondering when you'd show up."

She moved into position beside him, taking up a similar stance. The scent of her light perfume wrapped around him. Despite the fact they both stood looking out at the gardens, he knew she wasn't admiring the shrubs or the planters overflowing with roses. He had her complete attention.

"I was surprised to see you at my brother's wedding."

He glanced at her then, and she returned the gesture. Their gazes met. While he couldn't see her face behind the white mask she wore, it was hard to miss the cold indifference in her light blue eyes. He vowed to change that. He'd waited long enough for her, and he was no longer a young man. "My closest friend finally weds, and you didn't expect me to be there?"

She lifted a shoulder in a casual shrug but said nothing. She didn't have to.

Her brother, Brantford, had told him he was marrying for expediency, but the fact that he'd chosen to attach himself to someone whose family had fallen into social ruin spoke volumes. His friend hadn't said as much, but Castlefield could tell the woman in question meant something to him. More than Brantford wanted to admit. So Castlefield had agreed to stand at his friend's side during the marriage ceremony and hadn't pressed for details. He also hadn't questioned how Brantford had known he was in town when he'd only just arrived in London. The man knew everything.

Indiscreet laughter floated up from the hidden pathways of the gardens. The music inside the ballroom spilled out onto the balcony and concealed most of the noise caused by the lovers meeting under the cover of darkness, but the sound was unmistakable.

The season was drawing to a close, and as always, society seemed almost desperate to wring every drop of enjoyment from the time that remained. Especially those who had yet to secure matches. Which meant he'd been the object of much attention over the past week as he prowled the various events, looking for Ellen.

She was staying with her brother, but now that

Brantford had left town with his new wife, Castlefield knew she'd never accept a house call from him. So in order to see her, he'd had to attend the various balls and routs, waiting for her to decide to join the game. And that was problematic—although her attendance was much sought after, she rarely went out in public anymore. Indeed, she'd kept him waiting for the past week, but Castlefield had hoped tonight's masquerade would provide the perfect backdrop for their meeting.

He forced his thoughts away from the reason for Ellen's absence from society and turned to face her. She mirrored his movement.

Castlefield took in her outfit—a violet evening dress that complemented her fair coloring and dared to hug her curves just a little too closely. She'd come prepared to make an impression, and she'd succeeded. "You look beautiful, as ever."

Her eyes narrowed a fraction before she hid the telltale sign that she was annoyed. "I wasn't aware you cared one way or the other for my appearance. I certainly don't care for your opinion on the matter."

He couldn't stop the corner of his mouth from twitching in amusement. "I don't believe that to be true."

She turned away and looked out over the garden again. Muffled voices in the distance revealed that more than one couple were taking advantage of the darkness and lush greenery for a rendezvous. They'd be too busy with their own activities to pay attention to the two people standing a respectable distance from one another on the balcony.

"You're free to believe whatever you desire. Heaven knows, I could never change your mind about anything."

"We're not children any longer. Surely you can see past the actions of a callow youth."

"No, of course not. Why should I care that my best friend told me he no longer had time for silly girls?"

"We were twelve when that happened. And in my defense, you'd put a snake in my bed the evening before."

She allowed herself to smile then. "I must admit, that still amuses me. But you deserved it."

He said nothing since they both knew why she'd acted out. Their parents had been friends, and being of an age, he and Ellen had grown up together and spent many summers at his family's estate near Brighton. She hadn't been happy when he'd started spending more time with her brother, who was two years younger. Once Brantford was old enough to be deemed interesting by Castlefield, they'd begun to exclude her from their adventures. He'd never told her what had precipitated that action. He'd overheard a conversation between their parents wherein they'd discussed their hopes that his and Ellen's friendship would lead to a union when they were older. At the time, the very thought had horrified him, and so he'd pushed her away.

Ellen had made no bones about her displeasure with Castlefield and Brantford. But since she adored her younger brother, Castlefield had been the one to bear the brunt of that resentment.

But enough time had passed, and it was time to make his intentions known. "I'd like to propose that we begin anew."

The look she gave him was inscrutable, and he wished he could see more of her face than just her eyes through the white mask. He suspected she was trying to discern whether he had any ulterior motives. She'd never trust that his words were sincere. She'd been through too much, especially during her marriage to Laughton, to ever take a man's word at face value.

"Surely a man of your station can withstand a few rumors. While I find them vastly entertaining, I harbor no illusion they've done you any real harm."

If he were trying to find a suitable bride, he'd disagree with that sentiment. The whispers about his debauchery served to keep most marriage-minded mamas at bay. Those who didn't care about the rumors, whether because they wanted access to his sizable fortune or because the salacious on-dit intrigued them, weren't of any interest to him for anything beyond a short-term liaison.

No, there was only one woman who'd held his

interest for several years, and unfortunately it was the one standing before him now. The one who disliked him at best and who would no doubt hate him if she knew the truth about what he'd done.

But that didn't mean he was willing to quit the field. It was time for Ellen to learn he was the only man who could make her happy. She'd never accept his courtship, but he'd known her long enough to know she couldn't resist a challenge.

"I probably shouldn't admit this, certainly not to you, but I've decided it's time for me to settle down."

Ellen tilted her head to the side. "I wasn't aware you were courting anyone."

He watched her closely as he replied. "I haven't been, but that's about to change."

Ellen didn't seem disturbed by his announcement. "I don't know why you're telling me this, but I have to admit to being curious about the woman in question. Surely it's not someone attending the ball tonight?" She gave her head a small shake as though that thought displeased her.

"Actually, she is present tonight, but she isn't aware of my interest. I'll be announcing my intentions soon."

"Just like that? And what do you expect will happen? That she'll fall at your feet?" She gave a wry laugh. "Of course she will. There are no innocent young misses here tonight. You've probably already had half the women in that room."

He took heart from her statement. It might just have been a simple observation, but he told himself the thought that he'd been with other women clearly annoyed her.

"Oh, I don't expect it to go quite as smoothly as that. In fact, I believe I'll have a devil of a time convincing her to accept my suit."

Her brows rose at that. "This I will have to witness. I'll just slip inside now and find a clear vantage point of the room. I don't suppose you'll give me a hint?"

He glanced away but could feel her gaze wandering over his face, though his black domino covered enough of his features that she wouldn't be able to see what he was thinking. He allowed a corner of his mouth to lift. "As it turns out, you don't have to go anywhere." He turned to meet her eyes again and lowered his voice. "She's on the balcony."

Any other woman would have gazed wildly about, unable to rein in her curiosity. But Ellen had long since mastered the art of restraint. Ever so casually, she shifted position until she was leaning against the balustrade. While holding herself still, she allowed her eyes to roam over the large lit area. They were still alone, and she turned back to face him with a small huff of annoyance.

"I should have known you were playing games. Is it even true that you have your sights set on some poor woman?"

"Oh, it's definitely true. In fact, I'm looking at her right now."

The way Ellen's eyes widened in disbelief would have been comical if it didn't cause more than a slight sting. He smiled and folded his arms across his chest, preparing for her verbal assault.

"I don't find you amusing. Why don't you go and harass some other woman?"

"If memory serves, you were the one who approached me."

Her lips tightened a fraction as she struggled with her temper. "I'll remedy that right now."

Well, that had gone as disastrously as he'd expected. Fortunately, he wasn't above using Ellen's friendship with his sister to his benefit.

"Jane will be in town tomorrow."

Ellen remained impassive for several seconds before saying, "It's a little late, is it not?"

"She's only staying for a few days before heading down to the estate in Sussex."

"I'm sure she and Lord Eddings will have a pleasant time." She gave him a brief curtsy, saying, "If you'll excuse me, we've no doubt caused more than enough tongues to wag being out here alone. While that won't hurt your reputation, I'd rather not have my name aligned with yours should anyone recognize me."

He frowned at her cool dismissal. This was not

how he'd expected his revelation to go. "She wants to repair your friendship."

Ellen looked away, but from the stiff set of her jaw it was clear the news wasn't welcome. Her reaction confused him more than a little. He knew very well why Jane had needed to distance herself from the woman she'd once considered an older sister, but he hadn't realized just how hurt Ellen had been.

"I'm not sure we can be friends again."

Her words were short, clipped. He was missing something. This was more than just Ellen feeling hurt because they were no longer close. The woman before him seemed angry. He was fairly certain she had no idea what had taken place a few years earlier. If she had, it wouldn't be Jane with whom she was angry but him.

"Jane regrets the distance that has grown between you."

Ellen laughed, a short bitter sound. "Does she also regret having an affair with my husband?"

"What?" The word exploded from him before he could hold it back. A quick glance told him they were still alone on the balcony and no one was watching them through the garden doors.

When he turned back to Ellen, the sheen of tears in her eyes was unmistakable. He wanted to strangle Laughton. It was a pity Ellen's husband was already dead.

"Did Laughton tell you that?"

She gave a small nod, refusing to meet his eyes.

"And you believed him?"

"Not at first. But I went to see Jane, to warn her that Laughton was spreading rumors about her. I didn't think it was possible. Oh, I know my husband was more than capable of carrying out an affair with someone I considered a sister. Jane had hardly been the first woman with whom he'd dallied. But I didn't think it possible she would betray me in that way. I thought he was just striking out to hurt me."

"Jane wasn't having an affair with your husband." He barely restrained himself from swearing.

"She refused to see me. That was all the confirmation I needed."

He took her chin in his grip and guided her face back to him. She didn't resist, and he could see the hurt swimming in her eyes. That she wasn't trying to hide the emotion from him said more than words ever could about the depth of her pain.

"Jane was going through a very difficult time. She…" He had to struggle to keep his voice even as he continued. "She was carrying Hope at the time, and she almost lost her. The doctor had her on strict bed rest, and she didn't want to see anyone. It was a dark time for her, and she could barely even look at me."

"So she and Laughton…"

He gave his head a sharp shake. "Absolutely not. She… wasn't comfortable around your husband.

And as you said, she would never betray your friendship."

"You can't be certain—"

"Believe me, Ellen. There is nothing in this world about which I am more certain."

They stood like that for several long moments. She seemed to realize he was stroking her cheek with his thumb almost at the same time he did. With a visible swallow, she took a step back, and he allowed his hand to fall to his side.

"I'm more than a little relieved to hear that."

Castlefield wished he wasn't wearing gloves. What he wouldn't give to have felt the smoothness of her skin under his touch. He curled his hand and admonished himself for overstepping too soon. If he wasn't careful, he'd drive Ellen away from London before he had a chance to change her mind about how well the two of them would suit.

"I've promised to take her and the children to the Tower in two days' time so they can visit the royal menagerie. If he can manage it, Eddings will also be there."

Ellen had always gotten along with Jane's husband, and with their two children, they'd make a large enough group that she could convince herself she'd be able to ignore him during the outing. He'd laid down the bait, now he just had to wait to see if she'd take it.

"It would be nice to see Jane again. Heavens,

Henry must be so grown up now. And I haven't even met Hope."

He held back the desire to press the invitation. Any prodding from him would have her running in the other direction.

"I suppose I'll have to tolerate your presence?"

He inclined his head.

"And you'll give up this nonsense about courting me? I don't find it amusing being on the receiving end of one of your jokes."

"I would never make light of such an important matter."

Ellen sighed. "I don't know what you're trying to do. You can't be serious."

He met her gaze evenly, willing her to see just how earnest he was about the two of them.

Her eyes narrowed. "Fine, I'll join you. But I'm doing this because I miss my friendship with your sister."

It took every ounce of willpower he possessed not to say anything as she turned to leave. But internally, anticipation of the chase ahead surged.

CHAPTER 2

AFTER HIS CUSTOMARY early breakfast the next morning, Castlefield proceeded to his study where he hoped to distract himself with the reports sent by the steward of his country seat.

He'd dreamed of Ellen all night. Scene after scene where she danced just out of reach. Tempting him by coming close enough for him to catch the scent of her perfume before allowing herself to be whisked away by another masked man. He hadn't seen the man's face, but he knew that if he tore away the mask, he'd find it was her deceased husband.

It was difficult to banish the unsettling dreams from his mind, but he forced himself to look over the list of repairs his steward was undertaking.

He glanced up when the door to his study opened after a quick knock. His sister stepped into the room. It was early for her to be at his town house, but the staff knew she was welcome to come and go as she pleased.

"I shouldn't have to invade your inner sanctum to see my own brother. You're working much too hard, Charles."

Castlefield set aside the report and removed his reading glasses, tossing them onto the neatly organized surface. He'd only recently started needing to wear glasses when he read and hated how old they made him feel. He was only two-and-thirty. Surely too young for such an obvious sign that the years were passing far too quickly.

"I'm just trying to keep abreast of matters. The improvements needed at the country estate seem to be never ending."

"Is everything fine? I know Father left you with more than a handful when he passed away, but I always assumed he left the estate in order. Still, we both know that was a bad time. I was scarcely aware of what was happening around me."

Castlefield waved his hand, indicating she should make herself comfortable in the guest chair that was positioned on the other side of his desk for her visits.

"There's nothing to concern yourself with. Fortunately, the estate is large enough that it could withstand a little neglect. But improvements need to be made to ensure that continues to be the case."

Jane's shoulders slumped. "Should I let you return to it? I hate to be a burden—"

"You could never be a burden." He hated that she could think such a thing. His sister had never been one to doubt her worth until recently. Just one more crime he could lay at the feet of Ellen's deceased husband.

Jane's hands were bound tightly together in her lap, and he knew what she wanted to ask before she spoke. "Have you had an opportunity to speak to Ellen yet?"

"As a matter of fact, I ran into her last night. She's agreed to join us on our outing tomorrow."

Jane's face lit up. "I'm so pleased. But…" She gave her head a small shake before continuing. "I was so unbearably rude to her during that time, turning her away when she came to visit. I'm still not certain I haven't ruined our friendship forever."

He hated bringing up the past, but his sister needed to know what Ellen's husband had told her. Jane had been fragile for so long. She seemed to have regained her vigor and positive outlook over the past year, but he still felt the almost overwhelming need to shelter her from any negativity.

"I need to tell you something, but I don't want to upset you."

Jane sighed. "Did you have to coax her into giving me another chance? I knew it. Of course Ellen would hate me after the way I kept her at a distance."

"She doesn't hate you. But apparently over the past two years…" He had to force himself to continue when he saw the way Jane braced herself for whatever he was about to tell her. He rose from his seat and lowered himself into a crouch next to her chair. "Laughton told her that the two of you had an affair. Understandably, that news hurt Ellen. Not because her husband had betrayed her since she already knew he wasn't faithful." Castlefield ran his hand through his hair at his sister's gasp of outrage. He hated the fact that he had to mention that bastard's name again in his sister's presence. "He wielded your friendship with Ellen like a weapon, using you to hurt her. And since you weren't willing to give him what he wanted, he lied to her."

Jane's face had paled as he spoke, and he braced himself for her reaction. But instead of falling into tears as she would have done when this whole thing with Ellen's husband had happened, she gave a shaky laugh.

"Of course he did. It wasn't enough to try to force himself on me..." She took several deep breaths before she could continue, and he reached out to hold one of her hands. She tightened her grip in silent thanks. "Did you tell her the truth?"

"No, it isn't my place to share that with her." He released her hand and rose. "When you turned her away after she came to call, she took that as confirmation that her husband had been telling the truth. I told her that you weren't seeing anyone because you'd been placed on bed rest. It is up to you whether you want to share everything that happened. For now it is enough that the two of you take that first step toward healing your friendship." He smiled as he remembered Ellen's relief at the news Jane hadn't betrayed her. "She loves you like a sister, you know. I'm sure it will be good for her to have you back in her life."

Jane stood and smiled in return. "She wouldn't be only in my life."

"Not this again," Castlefield said with a small shake of his head.

"Can you blame me for wanting to see my brother happy? You hid it from everyone else, but I know how unhappy you were when Ellen married."

"I was young and stupid back then. By the time I realized the friend I'd pushed away had grown into a beautiful young woman whom I wanted to grow close to again, it was too late. She already hated me and was betrothed to another."

Jane looked away and fell silent for a moment. When she met his gaze again, he could see the telltale traces of sadness their conversation had stirred up in his sister.

"I wish you had decided to pursue her back then and forced her to break their engagement. I worry about what Laughton did to her while they were married."

All sorts of hateful images sprang to Castlefield's mind, images that he couldn't quite push away. "I do

19

as well, but we both know I wouldn't have been able to change her mind."

"And now? Please don't tell me you've given up on her."

"Never," he said with a confidence he was far from feeling. "I've waited long enough for Ellen."

Jane gave him a quick hug before stepping back. "Good. I'll enjoy having her as a sister when you win her heart."

"That outcome is far from certain, but I'm going to do everything in my power to make it happen."

CHAPTER 3

*E*LLEN WAS OF TWO MINDS that morning as the carriage rumbled along the streets of London toward the Tower. She couldn't deny she was excited to see Jane Eddings again. Far too many years had passed since she'd spoken to the woman who'd been like a younger sister to her.

She hated that her husband had succeeded in making her believe the worst of her friend. She knew Laughton had no qualms about having an affair with one of her friends. As she'd mentioned to Castlefield, it was no secret that her husband wasn't faithful in their marriage. But it had hurt her more than she thought possible when she believed Jane had betrayed her in such a fashion. She should have realized her husband was lying, striking out to hurt her. But she'd allowed herself to doubt their friendship when Jane had refused to see her.

What she hated most of all was the knowledge she hadn't been there for her friend when Jane had needed her. She must have gone through a very dark time indeed if she hadn't wanted to see anyone. And she could understand why she'd named her daughter Hope.

That's what Ellen had now. Hope that they'd be able to resurrect the tattered remains of their friendship.

If only Castlefield wasn't in the picture. She hated to admit just how much he'd rattled her at the masquerade. Normally she wouldn't be surprised that he'd tease her by telling her he wanted to court her. Such was the nature of their relationship after all, and she could have handled such teasing.

No, what bothered her most was her suspicion he might have told her the truth. Castlefield intended to court her, and that thought left her more than a little unsettled.

There was a time when she would have been thrilled with that prospect. Even though they'd needled each other for years whenever their families visited one another—and heaven knew, that was often since their parents were the best of friends—Ellen had started to develop an awareness of him that went beyond friendship as they grew older.

She'd known him as Charles then, despite the fact that everyone, even her brother, called him by his courtesy title of Haliburton.

But then Viscount Laughton had swept her off her feet, and she'd allowed herself to believe he loved her. It hadn't taken her long to discover any love he'd professed to feel for her was a sham. The real Laughton was cruel, and she'd suffered more than a little while under his control until she'd asked her brother to teach her how to defend herself against her husband's greater strength.

She owed Brantford everything. Those lessons had finally convinced her husband that she would no longer endure the bruises he inflicted on her whenever he took his husbandly rights. And she'd cheered inwardly when he stopped visiting her bed and found relief elsewhere.

She'd felt a twinge of guilt that he might be inflicting his rough hands on other women but told herself that Laughton wouldn't risk exposure in that way. He'd successfully courted her with sweet words, after all, and had even kept his darker desires at bay for the first year of their marriage. No, Laughton wouldn't have hurt any of those other women the way he'd hurt her. She had to believe that.

Ellen was jostled from her morbid thoughts when the carriage slowed. She took a deep breath and tried to look forward to the day ahead. She'd never actually visited the area that housed the menagerie. She'd been to the Tower two weeks before with her brother and the young woman who was now his wife, but the reason for their visit had been a grim one. Rose's father was currently being held in the Tower after confessing to treason. Even now, her brother was attempting to gather evidence to prove the man hadn't committed the crime but had confessed because the lives of his wife and daughter were in danger. She knew if such evidence existed, Brantford would find it.

The carriage stopped, and a footman—probably assigned by her brother to watch over her while he was away—opened the door to help her down and would probably follow her during the day. She hadn't decided whether to be annoyed with her brother, but given his line of work she couldn't blame him for being overprotective. Still, she'd proven to be an adept student at self-defense and could handle herself in most circumstances.

She was only a few minutes late, but she hadn't wanted to arrive early. She hated waiting for others to arrive. Jane and Castlefield had always been punctual in the past, but the former was now a mother to two young children. In all likelihood, they hadn't yet learned the value of being on time.

She scanned the modest crowd of people and spied the others waiting by the drawbridge that led to the Lion Tower. Castlefield and Jane were speaking and hadn't noticed her arrival yet.

Much to her annoyance, her gaze settled first on Castlefield. She told herself it was only to be expected since he was over six feet in height and exuded a commanding air. With his dark hair and undeniable good looks, it was impossible to be indifferent to his presence. Not that she'd ever admit that to him.

Her gaze moved to Jane, and she couldn't stop the smile that spread over her face as she took in the petite, dark-haired figure of Castlefield's sister. It appeared that Jane's husband hadn't been able to join them. But what struck her most was how much Jane's children had grown.

Henry would now be six. She'd last seen him when he was four, and she'd never met Hope, who would be just shy of two years of age. A servant, no doubt the children's nurse, hovered in the background. Ellen wasn't surprised that Hope was perched on her mother's hip—Jane had always enjoyed carrying Henry when he was younger. But she hadn't expected to see Henry's hand in Castlefield's.

Castlefield noticed her then and said something to his sister. Ellen's heart lurched when she saw the emotions that crossed Jane's face. Happiness first, tinged with an air of uncertainty. Ellen vowed to do away with that second emotion right away.

She moved toward the small group and gave Jane a quick hug, including her daughter in the embrace.

"I am so happy to see you," she said, hating the tears that threatened to fall. She forced them back and turned to the child in her friend's arms. "And who is this beautiful young woman? I don't believe we've had the pleasure of being introduced."

"This is Hope Ellen," Jane said, not bothering to dash away the tear that even now tracked down her face.

Shocked, Ellen's gaze moved to meet her friend's. "You named her after me?"

Jane gave her a one-armed hug before stepping back. "You are the strongest woman I know. I wanted to give my daughter someone to look up to."

Emotion unfurled in Ellen's chest, and she had to look away to gather her strength lest she embarrass herself and prove just how wrong Jane was.

She turned toward the little boy at Castlefield's side and lowered herself into a crouch. "And you must be Henry. The last time I saw you, you were only this tall." She lifted her hand to indicate his former height, smiling as she remembered the way he used to call her Aunt Ellen. She extended her hand to give him a handshake and was surprised when the boy released Castlefield's hand and gave her a quick hug before stepping back again.

"Can we go see the lions now?"

Ellen laughed, grateful that the tense atmosphere had lightened thanks to Henry's enthusiasm.

"No dashing off," Castlefield said, bringing a frown to his nephew's face.

"I'll make sure he doesn't get too far ahead of us," the nurse said. She held her hand out, and with an audible sigh, the boy grasped it.

Castlefield smiled down at the woman and Ellen

felt a slight twinge of annoyance at the way she beamed in response. She was younger than Ellen had suspected after stepping out of the carriage, certainly younger than Ellen's own thirty-two years of age. And quite attractive in a youthful, fresh-faced way.

Ellen looked away, refusing to betray her emotions. She was only here for Jane, to reclaim the friendship her husband had done his utmost to sever. Castlefield's actions were no concern to her. He could sleep with every female servant he met for all she cared. Heaven knew her husband had done the same.

She took a deep breath and pushed back the melancholy mood that threatened to settle over her, telling herself it had to do with thoughts of her unhappy marriage and not the man who had turned to watch her.

"Where should we begin?" she asked, knowing Jane's son wouldn't be able to hold back his enthusiasm.

"The lions!" Henry exclaimed, tugging on his nurse's hand and trying to lead them to the bridge.

"By all means," Castlefield said with a chuckle. He indicated that the women should precede him.

Of course, Henry had to be in the lead, so he and his nurse led the small group. Ellen took her place at Jane's side while Castlefield followed. She tried to ignore the sensation that his eyes were on her as they crossed over the drawbridge to the tower that housed the royal menagerie.

Ellen threaded her arm through her friend's free arm and smiled down at Hope, whose head was leaning on her mother's shoulder. "She's going to get heavy."

"I know," Jane replied. "She woke very early this morning thanks to her excited brother. I suspect she'll sleep through most of this morning's visit. Fortunately, Charles can carry her if I get tired."

Ellen's eyes widened. "Castlefield? Would he stoop so low as to do the work of a servant?"

Jane laughed. "I see you're still needling him. You know as well as I that my brother isn't like that. He actually enjoys spending time with his niece and nephew."

"If you say so."

Jane's eyes softened. "I've missed you so much. I cannot express to you how happy I was to learn you'd be joining us today."

Any lingering doubts Ellen might have had vanished in the face of her friend's happiness. "We have a lot of time to make up."

As promised, Hope fell asleep almost as soon as Castlefield paid the keeper who was to guide them on their tour. The girl opened her eyes when the lion roared but closed them again almost immediately, a contented smile on her face.

Jane glanced over at her brother, who stepped forward to take Hope from her arms.

Jane sighed. "Soon she won't be content to be

held and will be running everywhere, just like her brother."

The two of them glanced at where Henry stood before the lion's cage, his hand still firmly held by his nurse. He peppered the keeper with questions about what the animals ate and if anyone at the Tower had ever been attacked.

Castlefield moved to stand next to the small boy, ruffling his dark hair with his free hand. Hope slept in his arms, looking for all the world like she belonged there. At the domestic sight, Ellen's heart squeezed with an emotion she refused to acknowledge.

"He's very good with them." She felt a twinge of guilt for spreading all those rumors about him. This was a man who should be wed. It was clear he'd make a wonderful father. Whether he'd also make a good husband... Well, she refused to dwell on those thoughts.

Whatever the future held, Ellen was certain of one thing. She would never again allow herself to be tied to a man who held absolute control over her. She'd made that mistake once, marrying for love when her younger brother had voiced doubts about Laughton's suitability, and it would never happen again.

She and Jane fell into an easy camaraderie, their lifelong closeness doing much to ease the strain from the two-year rift in their friendship. And it was easier being near Castlefield with so many others present.

As they neared the end of their visit, Ellen wasn't

surprised to see her former nemesis hand Hope, who was now awake, to the nurse. Jane stepped forward to take Henry's hand, preventing the boy from racing back to see the lions, which he'd proclaimed were his favorite. The only disappointment had been the fact that monkeys were no longer housed in the Tower.

Castlefield moved to her side to take Jane's place.

The shift was seamless, and she wouldn't have noticed their casual movements if her brother hadn't trained her to be on alert to everything that was happening around her. She wouldn't be surprised if Castlefield had planned this with his sister ahead of time. He'd made it clear when they'd last spoken that he intended to pursue her, and she'd been waiting for him to act on that declaration.

He bent and spoke quietly. At the low timbre of his voice so near to her ear, a strange emotion came over her. She refused to examine why that would be.

"It means the world to Jane that you agreed to accompany us today."

She glanced at him, keeping her tone even. "Your presence wasn't necessary for this visit."

Castlefield raised a brow. "Who would have carried my adorable but surprisingly heavy niece if I hadn't been here?"

Ellen allowed him to see her amusement at his feigned innocence. "You're good with them. I wouldn't have believed it."

He gave her a searching stare. "Not all men are villains, Ellen."

Uncomfortable, she looked away. "My experience has shown me that isn't entirely true."

He gave his head a small shake. "You haven't been keeping company with the right crowd then. You remember how doting Jane's husband was, and that certainly hasn't changed since you last saw him. She'd tell you just how happy she is in her marriage, and she wouldn't be doing so to save face."

He was referring to her own marriage, of course, and annoyance flared as she remembered doing just that with him—pretending she was content with her situation—when he'd asked her a few years after she'd wed if she was happy. This conversation was becoming far too personal for her comfort, and she sought to put some emotional distance between them.

"Henry calls you Uncle Charles."

A small vee formed between Castlefield's brows. "What else would he call me?"

"Your Grace?"

Instead of being annoyed, Castlefield laughed. "That might have been how you were raised, but you know full well my parents never demanded such circumspect formality when we were en famille. Jane and I have continued that tradition, preferring the closeness that arises when one doesn't demand their relatives treat them like strangers."

"And Lord Eddings agrees?"

Castlefield smiled. "Eddings does whatever his wife wants."

A pang of what Ellen could only assume was jealousy went through her at the matter-of-fact statement. She'd had to fight for every bit of consideration in her own marriage. When they were well and truly bound together, Laughton had ceased all pretense of caring about his wife's desires. He'd barely cared about her physical well-being, after all.

A tense silence settled between them. Several seconds passed before Castlefield spoke.

"If memory serves, you used to call me Charles."

Yes, she had. But then everything had changed. "We used to be friends."

"I'd like to go back to that. I miss our friendship."

His expression was so earnest, his words echoing a similar nostalgia she hadn't even known existed within her. If only she could trust him. But too many years had passed, and she'd started too many rumors about his unsuitability to believe he only wanted friendship. If she were in his place, she'd want revenge, and what better way to attain it than to lull your enemy into a false sense of security?

"I'm not sure we can ever be friends again."

"Ellen—"

She stopped and turned to face him. The others in their group continued on. When she was certain they were no longer close enough to hear, she spoke. "What exactly are you planning?"

His smile was a sad one, and Ellen had to remind herself that her own husband had been a convincing actor. No one, least of all her, had had any inkling as to his true personality until after they'd wed.

"I never should have allowed you to marry Laughton."

Ellen examined him closely for a few moments. "How much did my brother tell you about our marriage?" Almost as soon as she'd asked the question, she gave her head a sharp shake. "Never mind—I don't want you to answer that. But we both know you had little choice in the matter. I thought myself madly in love with him, and my father approved the match. Nothing could have stopped it."

It seemed as though Castlefield was about to discuss the matter further, but instead he changed the subject. "Let us put the past behind us. I'd like us to return to our former friendship. And then…" He took hold of one of her hands. "I wasn't lying when I said I intend to court you."

"Is that what today was all about? You're using your family to get close to me? I assume you intend to make a laughingstock of me. Make me believe that you care for me and then toss me aside. What rumors would you spread about me then? Would I have the privilege of hearing myself referred to as the unwanted widow?"

Her anger was real. Instead of chagrin at being

caught out, however, Castlefield straightened to his full height.

"I would never treat you in such a manner. Laughton might have been cruel, but I care too much about your feelings to ever mock you in such a way."

She watched him carefully, expecting to see some crack in his demeanor. "Even though society calls you the unsuitable duke solely because of me?"

A corner of Castlefield's mouth lifted in what appeared to be genuine amusement. "Funny thing that. The more rumors circulated about me, the more sought after I became in certain circles. Oh, the parents of all the young girls that are paraded about every year made sure to keep their daughters away from me, but those women with a few years of experience…" He shrugged. "Let's just say I'm very popular with widows. I've also had my share of invitations when various members of the *ton* found themselves alone because their husbands had gone hunting, but I've never been one to cuckold another man."

He'd rendered her speechless. Never in a million years had she expected that some of the very rumors she thought she was fabricating were, in actuality, true. When he lifted his hand, it took every ounce of strength she possessed not to flinch. Her days of flinching before a raised fist were over. Besides, she soon realized that he wasn't about to strike her. Instead, he seemed to caress her chin, and she realized that her mouth had dropped open.

She stepped back from him. "I am not one of those widows."

"I know, which means you are all the more worthy of my attention. You always have been, and I regret that I ever made you think otherwise."

Ellen shook her head. "My defenses are legendary. You should quit now and direct your attention elsewhere. If it helps in your quest to find a bride, you should know that I no longer intend to spread any rumors about you. Even if it turns out that most of them are true."

"I've always enjoyed a challenge, and I know the same can be said of you."

Their gazes met and held for several long moments, and Ellen found herself unsure what to say to this man who was staring down at her with dark intent. Fortunately, she received a reprieve in the form of one small, very rambunctious little boy.

"Uncle Charles, we've been waiting ages for you. Mama says we can have an ice at Gunter's now, but we have to wait for you to join us."

Castlefield laughed and ruffled his nephew's hair again. "Far be it from me to come between my favorite nephew and his well-deserved treat for good behavior." He took the boy's hand and looked back at Ellen. "Will you be joining us?"

Ellen needed to retreat, so she shook her head. "Not today."

"Another time then. Soon."

He allowed Henry to drag him away, and Ellen followed. She noticed Jane's curious expression but carefully steered the conversation back to some of the more exotic animals they'd seen during their tour of the menagerie. She took her leave when they crossed the bridge and left the Tower behind them.

Alone, as she told herself she preferred to be, she allowed the footman to help her into her waiting carriage and returned to her brother's town house.

CHAPTER 4

THE CONVERSATION she'd had with Castlefield weighed heavily on Ellen's mind that evening and into the following morning, probably because she hated any reminder of her unhappy marriage. It shouldn't bother her anymore—Laughton had died in a hunting accident two years ago. She'd followed the customary mourning period of one year, but secretly she'd been relieved to be free from her marriage. They'd been wed only ten years, but it had felt like a lifetime.

For the past year she'd been working with her brother, donning the disguise of an older woman and acting as a lady's maid on several occasions when he needed someone to keep watch over women who were either under the Crown's protection or under their scrutiny. Of course, Brantford had also made sure to place several footmen in those households to ensure her safety and that of her charges, but Ellen had practiced long and hard to be able to defend herself in most situations. That she'd once been totally powerless, completely under the power of her husband, was something she tried not to think about.

She hated being idle, but at the moment she found herself with little to do. Brantford and his new bride were away from London, following a lead that could prove her sister-in-law's father hadn't committed treason. Ellen hoped with all her heart that they'd find that proof. She liked Rose very much, and it would break the young woman's heart if her father was hanged for the crime, especially since Rose was convinced he was innocent.

Her boredom as she waited for news from her brother had led her to bait Castlefield, arranging to run into him at the masquerade three days earlier. It was one of her favorite pastimes when they were both in town. But he'd turned the tables on her, putting her on the defensive, which was a situation that couldn't be allowed to stand.

She found herself pacing through her brother's town house that morning. Jane had mentioned she planned to visit, and Ellen found it impossible to sit still as she waited. Despite the fact she was looking forward to her friend's visit, her thoughts centered on Castlefield's motives for trying to convince her he wanted to court her. They'd needled one another for years, but her childhood friend had never been cruel. And yet the possibility he was telling her the truth seemed equally impossible to believe.

She'd just have to ask Jane her opinion on the matter. If Castlefield had changed, if he'd become the kind of man who would have no qualms about hurting a woman emotionally—the kind of man her husband had been—she needed to know. She was always guarded around men, especially if they showed an interest in her, but her past friendship with Castlefield was proving to be problematic. She found it impossible to believe he'd go to such lengths to get back at her for the rumors she'd spread about him, not when it was clear those rumors hadn't hurt him in the least.

She'd wandered to the back of the house and was gazing out at the garden when the butler informed her that her guest had arrived. Ellen instructed him to bring refreshments and hurried to the drawing room. She'd seen Jane only yesterday, but they still had so much to catch up on.

Jane rose from her seat on the settee when Ellen swept into the room. Without a word, Ellen crossed over to her friend and gave her a quick but heartfelt hug.

Jane smiled at her when Ellen stepped back. "There are no children in our way today," she said. "Now we can become properly reacquainted."

Ellen waited for Jane to sit again before taking the

seat next to her. The past still weighed heavily on her mind, and they needed to deal with the reason for the distance that had grown between them so they could move past it.

"I am sorry for doubting your friendship. What did Castlefield tell you?"

Jane stiffened and for a moment, and Ellen didn't think she was going to reply.

Finally, after what seemed like forever, Jane gave her head a sharp shake. "I shouldn't be surprised that Lord Laughton told you the two of us were having an affair. It isn't true—"

Seeing her distress, Ellen rushed to reassure her. "I know. I should apologize for ever believing a word he had to say on the subject. He was so smug though, and when you wouldn't see me I feared the worse. I never should have doubted you."

Jane had looked away, and Ellen had the distinct impression she was missing something. Her friend's next words made her stomach drop.

"Your husband did approach me, but I turned him away."

Ellen reached for her Jane's hand and squeezed it. "I know. You would never betray me in such a fashion. Laughton…" Ellen hesitated, not sure how much to share. In the end, she decided that the subject of her husband was best left in the past. "Well, suffice it to say that he wasn't the best of husbands. I counted myself fortunate when he forgot all about me and moved on to other women. I'm not surprised he approached you. He made it a game to try to hurt me."

"I can't talk about this," Jane said, pulling her hand out of Ellen's grip and wrapping her arms around her midsection. "Shortly after he spoke to me, I had difficulty with my pregnancy…"

Her friend's voice broke, and Ellen felt like a monster for bringing up that terrible time.

"Hope is a darling little girl," she said, her voice soft. "I've always wanted a daughter. Of course, the best I can hope for now is that Brantford will have children so I can spoil my nieces and nephews. And if you'll allow it, I'd love to go back to being Aunt Ellen to your children."

Jane gave her a sly look, one that had Ellen tilting her head in question. "You could be Aunt Ellen in reality."

Ellen forced a laugh at Jane's statement. "Has Castlefield roped you into his charade that he's attempting to woo me?"

Jane shook her head. "It isn't a pretense, Ellen. He's in earnest."

Ellen was saved from replying when a footman arrived with tea and refreshments. She thanked the servant and lifted the pot to pour their tea. "You still take it with milk and sugar?"

Jane murmured her agreement and watched on in silence. Ellen was torn between wanting to change the subject and pressing Jane for the truth, but she couldn't decide what she would do with the information. In the end, Jane decided the matter for her.

"Charles is ready to settle down, and I honestly believe he wants to do so with you."

Ellen shook her head. "Your brother and I have too much negative history to make that possible. Besides, after my last marriage, I'm not likely to undertake another."

Jane gave her a look that was filled with such sympathy, such understanding, Ellen began to wonder whether there were secrets in her own marriage. But her next words had her doubting those thoughts.

"If anyone deserves to be happy, it's you," she said, reaching for Ellen's hand. "I want you to be as happy as I am. You should give Charles a chance."

Ellen searched her friend's face and came to the realization that Jane was absolutely convinced such a match was possible. A pang of remorse settled like a lead weight on her chest. Perhaps, in another lifetime, if Laughton hadn't been so cruel, she could have taken that chance. Heaven knew Castlefield was attractive, and the fact that her brother remained loyal to him spoke volumes. Brantford had always been a good judge of character. She should have heeded him when he expressed his displeasure about her betrothal to Laughton. Of course, she'd been young and had fancied herself in love, and that had been before Brantford had risen to his current position. She'd never imagined the man she was about to wed would raise a hand to her in anger.

Ellen decided to push aside all thoughts of men and concentrate on her rekindled friendship with the woman who had always been like a sister to her but would never become one in reality.

"Let's talk of other things," Ellen said. "We are neither one of us young girls anymore, seeking to catch the attention of an attractive man."

Jane's smile was sad, but she allowed Ellen to change the subject. She reached for a small cake and took a nibble, sighing with pleasure. "You remembered my weakness for sweets. I've had to banish them from my own house or I'd be twice as wide as I am now, but I've never been able to refuse when they're offered to me elsewhere."

Ellen laughed, her tension easing. "I have to tempt you to continue visiting me somehow."

Jane shook her head. "Never again will we allow anyone to come between us. Speaking of which… I'm not sure how to ask this now."

Ellen reached for the tray of sweets just as Jane was about to take another cake and held it out of reach. "If you want more of these, you'll stop hedging and come out with it."

"Fine," Jane said with a huff of mock annoyance.

"You remember how your family used to visit ours in Sussex every summer?"

"Of course. It was always the highlight of our year."

"It's been a few years, but I'd like to restart that tradition. In fact, that's where we're heading after my husband finishes his business here in London. We'll be staying at my brother's estate for a few weeks before heading out to Brighton where we've purchased our own home."

"Will Castlefield also be there?"

Jane tilted her head to one side. "That won't be a problem, I hope. I know the two of you used to squabble when you were younger, but you seemed to get along at the Tower."

Ellen couldn't help but wonder if this spontaneous invitation had been at Castlefield's urging. Despite the feeling that he was shifting pieces on an imaginary chessboard to further whatever goals he had in mind, she found herself tempted to accept. "I've missed those summer visits. But I'm hoping that my brother and his new wife will return to town soon, and I'd hate to not be here."

"I will be extending the invitation to them as well, of course." Her eyes widened in a plea, and Ellen returned the tray of sweets. Jane snatched another small cake and gave her a sheepish smile before continuing. "I still can't believe Brantford actually married! I was certain he'd remain a bachelor forever."

"You should see them together," Ellen said with a fond smile. "Brantford tries so hard to maintain his air of aloofness around Rose, but it's clear he cares for her. I'm so happy for him… for the two of them."

"Then I'll make sure to leave an invitation for him before we depart for Sussex. With any luck we'll see them before my husband and I depart for Brighton. Please say you'll join us."

Ellen hesitated. "Given the recent animosity between your brother and me, I'm not sure I should accept."

Jane's face fell, and Ellen couldn't help but feel a pang of guilt. Her friend didn't try to change her mind, not with words, but the expression of disappointment on her face did far more to convince her than mere words could have.

"All right," Ellen said, certain she would come to regret it. "I'll come down after you've all had a chance to settle in."

Jane gave her another quick hug. "Oh, we're going to have so much fun! And it will give you a chance to become acquainted with the children."

Her friend's enthusiasm was so contagious that Ellen found herself wanting to believe everything would be fine. Castlefield would give up his ill-conceived notion of the two of them marrying, and she'd regain her position of almost-sister within the family.

She didn't examine why that thought left her with a hint of remorse as she listened to Jane go on about all the things she had planned once she retired to her new home in Brighton in a few weeks' time.

CHAPTER 5

*C*ASTLEFIELD NEEDED to burn off his excess energy, so after sending his valet off with the carriage that carried his trunks that morning, he headed out to the stables.

The road from London to Sussex was well traveled this time of year, with many heading out to enjoy the weather at Brighton. There wasn't much chance of being waylaid by highwaymen, but just in case, he'd dressed in worn, dull-colored clothing. It would take him about four hours to travel by horseback, giving his valet just enough time to fuss over him before he joined his mother for dinner.

His mother, the Dowager Duchess of Castlefield, had taken to spending the entire year at the house in Sussex, leaving the country seat in the north to Castlefield during the winter months. He knew it was because she missed her husband a great deal. Their happiest memories were the summers they'd spent at the house in Sussex, and so he hadn't minded that she'd chosen to make it her permanent residence after his death.

And that led him back to thinking of his own future. He didn't want to dwell on events that might never come to pass, but he couldn't stop thinking about Ellen. Now, of course, he realized he'd been a fool. If he hadn't pushed her away when they were still little more than children, it was likely he and Ellen would have wed. By the time he realized the girl with whom he'd once been close friends had grown into a beautiful young woman, it was too late. She'd fallen in love with Laughton and had accepted his proposal.

Intellectually he knew he wasn't responsible for the hurt she must have suffered at his hands—no, the blame for that lay squarely on Laughton's shoulders—but how different could things have been if he hadn't ended their friendship? Those thoughts had haunted him for years. But now he was done waiting for Ellen.

He'd have to be cautious in his approach. He'd told her about his intentions, but he was fairly certain she didn't believe him. If she did, he suspected she'd already have run in the opposite direction. Buried herself at one of her brother's estates or, as was more likely, donned one of her disguises and attempted to blend in somewhere he wouldn't be able to find her.

He'd almost had heart failure when Brantford told him he'd employed Ellen on some of his missions since her husband's death. His friend had assured him she was more than capable of handling herself and that he made sure she was never in real danger. Still, the thought had kept Castlefield up more than a few nights.

He could ascribe the fact that she hadn't already disappeared to the knowledge that she wanted to make up for the years she'd missed with Jane and her family. That and her curiosity. Ellen always had an insatiable need to know everything that was happening. He knew that declaring himself as he'd done, especially since she wouldn't believe he was being earnest, would spark her interest as to his motives. But he'd have to proceed with caution from this point forward, keep her guessing so she wouldn't disappear.

Having to wait for her tested the limits of his patience since he couldn't shake the feeling this would be the only chance he'd have to win Ellen's trust. He ran through a number of strategies as his horse kept a steady canter. When he finally reached the estate, he was more determined than ever about his current course of action.

He didn't bother riding into the stables. With the arrival of his valet, his mother would know he was en route and would have informed the staff to be on the lookout for him. When he reached the long road leading up to the house, he could see her figure by the front door.

He left his horse in the capable hands of one of

the grooms who was also waiting nearby and went to greet his mother. She'd been a young woman when she had him and was still striking. However, her dark hair was now threaded with silver, and the beginnings of fine lines creased the skin around her eyes.

"You're early," she said, engulfing him in a hug.

He closed his eyes, content to bask in her warmth and love before pulling back and smiling down at her. In years past, his father would be standing by her side, but neither of them spoke of his absence. She'd want to talk about him later, but now was not a time for tears.

"Jane's coming down with the family tomorrow. She invited me to travel with them, but I couldn't wait."

His mother gave him a knowing smile. "Couldn't wait or didn't want to be cooped up with a rambunctious child who would no doubt be pestering you with questions the entire way?"

He didn't bother correcting her. While he knew many households had their children travel in separate carriages with their governess or nurse, that had never been the habit within their own family. Henry's exuberance didn't normally bother him, but he feared that in his current preoccupied state, he'd be less than patient with the boy. He wouldn't cease being on edge until Ellen arrived at the estate.

It was as if his mother had read his mind when she spoke again. "I'm so glad to hear that Ellen will be returning for a visit. It's been far too long since she and her brother were last here."

"Jane was excited. I hope it won't prove too much of an inconvenience. I know she also extended an invitation to Brantford and his new wife, but I don't know if they'll make it down."

He thought he'd kept his voice impassive, but there must have been something in his tone or in his expression that caused a speculative gleam to enter his mother's eyes. Of course, it could simply be that he was now two-and-thirty and his mother was eager to see him wed. Fortunately, she didn't press the subject.

"You should get settled. I'll see you at eight for dinner. That will give us a chance to talk before your sister's family arrives tomorrow."

He bent to press a kiss to his mother's cheek, then made his way inside. What he'd wanted to do was groan. *Talking* meant that his mother planned to question him about all aspects of his life. And it wouldn't take long for the conversation to turn to the subject of heirs.

CHAPTER 6

*E*LLEN HAD NOTHING with which to occupy her thoughts as her carriage traveled from London to Castlefield's estate in Sussex. She'd left early and tried to pass the time reading. But after remaining on the same page for some time as her thoughts continued to wander, she threw the book onto the dark cushions beside her in disgust.

It had been a long time since she'd had to deal with the sensation of nerves settling in the pit of her stomach. Not since she'd had to worry about what sort of mood her husband would be in. The past two years of calm since his passing had been a blessed relief, and she wasn't happy about the return of unsettled emotions.

At least these nerves weren't caused by fear, an emotion she knew all too well. Even when her husband stopped being rough with her physically—

and she could attribute that squarely to her brother's lessons in how to defend herself from an attack— she'd still had to deal with his dark moods and insults.

No, the reason butterflies currently rioted within her could be laid squarely at Castlefield's feet and sprang from his ridiculous declaration. She'd convinced herself in the week since Jane had called on her that he was toying with her, trying to get back at her for causing several of the rumors currently being spread about him. That she now felt a twinge of guilt about creating the on-dit about his voracious sexual appetites—a rumor that surely would guarantee no one would want to see their precious daughters wed him—proved just how much he'd unsettled her.

What bothered her most about the entire situation was that she couldn't stop wondering how Castlefield would go about trying to woo her. Would he be relentless in his pursuit, as Laughton had been in trying to win her heart? Or would he rely mainly on their shared childhood, trying to convince her that theirs was a logical union?

It was just after midday when the carriage slowed and drew to a halt before Castlefield's Sussex estate. Ellen took several deep breaths, attempting to push aside her nerves. They didn't disappear, but she was determined not to let them show. She wouldn't give Castlefield the upper hand in the latest battle of the war that waged between them.

When the carriage door opened, she half

expected to find him standing there, an insufferable smirk on his face. Instead, she looked into the impassive face of the footman who'd been accompanying her whenever she left the house and who had ridden alongside the carriage driver. She shook off her disappointment, telling herself she'd merely been looking forward to delivering a scathing setdown, and allowed the footman to help her.

Memories of all the summers she'd spent here had her smiling widely as she approached the main entrance. The house was smaller than the one at his country seat, but it was still impressive and had two wings. The last time she'd visited with her family was the year before she and Laughton had wed. Thirteen years had passed since that summer.

The door opened just as she reached it, and a wave of fondness hit her when she realized that Trenton still served as their butler. He allowed himself a slight upturning of his mouth before donning his impassive facade and stepping aside to allow her to enter. Waves of nostalgia swept over her, and she realized in that moment just how much she'd missed her family's yearly visits. After she'd wed, her husband had told her that he wasn't fond of sea air, and so her trips to Sussex had come to an end.

"It's good to see you, Trenton."

He responded by way of inclining his head, but Ellen could tell he was pleased to see her.

"The family is waiting for you in the morning room."

She thanked him and made her way down the airy hallway toward the back of the house. She couldn't help but feel as though she were coming home again. This house held so many happy memories of her childhood. Even later, when her brother and Castlefield would sneak off, leaving her behind, she'd passed the time thinking of ways to annoy them when they returned. She'd taken most of her anger out on Castlefield, however. Brantford had told her on numerous occasions that he'd wanted to wait for her, but his friend had insisted that Ellen would be bored tagging along after them. Her brother had been so earnest that she hadn't had the heart to remain angry with him.

Castlefield had been another matter since they'd been friends and companions their entire childhood. She had to hold back a smile as she recalled how many times he'd barged into her room, furious after finding yet another frog or snake in his bed. It was her favorite way to show him her displeasure, and she never tired of his outrage. She knew he wasn't afraid of the creatures—he was the one who'd taught her how to capture and handle them, after all—but he always took the opportunity to berate her.

The sound of laughter beckoned to her as she entered the morning room. It had always been her favorite room in the house, with tall windows along two walls that allowed the sun to stream in from morning to late afternoon. They showcased the garden just beyond, and she looked forward to strolling through them once again. Her gaze wasn't on that sight though, but rather on its occupants, when she stepped into the room.

Jane was seated on the floor next to her son, playing a game Ellen couldn't discern from a distance. The dowager duchess was seated in an armchair, working on a square of embroidery. A slight frown of concentration marked the space between her eyes. They hadn't noticed her silent arrival.

"I hope I'm not interrupting."

Three pairs of eyes moved to look at her, followed by Jane springing up from her position on the floor and crossing the room to embrace her. "We weren't expecting you until later this afternoon."

"I couldn't wait to join you and so left first thing this morning." She turned to face the dowager duchess, who had also risen from her seat. "Thank you for the invitation, Duchess," she said with a small curtsy.

The duchess reached out to take both her hands and gave them a slight squeeze before releasing them again. "You are always welcome here. It has been far too long since you last visited, and so much has changed."

Her gaze moved over to her grandson, a fond smile on her face. But Ellen knew she was referring more to all the losses their families had suffered over the past several years. Castlefield's father, Ellen's parents, and her husband. That she didn't mourn Laughton's passing wasn't something she'd ever say aloud, however.

"I couldn't believe how much Henry had changed when I saw him last week," Ellen said, doing her part to keep the conversation light. "He's almost a young man now."

Henry had abandoned his game and stood at his mother's side. "I remember you," he said. "We met at the Tower."

A pang pulled at her heart. Of course he wouldn't remember her from his earlier years. He'd only been four when Ellen and Jane had stopped speaking. But she vowed that before this visit was over, she would again become an honorary aunt in his eyes.

"Yes, we did," she said, crouching before him. "I seem to remember you had a younger sister. Have you hidden her away?" She feigned an exaggerated scowl.

Henry laughed, and the sound lifted her heart. "No. All Hope does is sleep all day."

Jane laid a hand on Henry's shoulder, her affection for her son clear. "Henry was vastly disappointed we didn't give him a brother."

"I have a younger brother," Ellen said.

Henry tilted his head to one side. "I'm sure he didn't sleep all day. Nurse says little boys always have so much energy."

"That might be true of boys who've reached the grand age of six. But even little boys take naps when they are as small as your sister."

The look on Henry's face told her he didn't believe her. She wanted to pull him into a hug but hesitated, not wanting to overstep her bounds.

Jane must have realized it. She gave Henry's shoulder a pat and said, "Give your Aunt Ellen a proper welcome."

Henry looked up at his mother and said in what was meant to be a whisper but fell far from that mark, "I forgot." He stepped forward and wrapped his little arms around her. Dismay at all the years she'd missed had Ellen hugging him longer that she'd expected, and soon he was squirming in her arms. When she released him and rose to stand, he returned to his game on the floor.

"I'll call for tea," the duchess said, moving to the bellpull that was hidden behind the curtains. "You must be famished."

Ellen inclined her head in thanks and turned back to Jane. "Where is everyone?"

She wouldn't come out and ask about Castlefield directly, but she was beginning to wonder if he'd changed his mind and remained in London. She ignored the disappointment caused by the thought, telling herself she'd miss the challenge of matching wits with the man. She certainly didn't want him attempting to court her, as he'd stated was his intention.

"Charles and my husband are hidden away in my brother's study. I'll send a footman to let them know you've arrived. I know my brother in particular will be happy to see you again."

Ellen didn't miss the gleam in Jane's eyes, and she wanted to groan. It seemed their conversation the week before had done little to dissuade Jane from believing she and Castlefield would make a match. She cast a quick glance at Jane's mother, whose expression was carefully neutral. Ellen didn't even want to imagine what thoughts were going through the older woman's mind.

The sound of voices coming from the hallway heralded the arrival of the two men and saved Ellen from having to address the subject.

When the men crossed the threshold, Jane moved to her husband's side and greeted him with a quick peck on the cheek.

"You're just in time," she said. "Ellen has arrived and we've rung for tea." She turned to face Ellen. "I know it's been a few years, but you remember my husband, Lord Eddings."

"Of course, my lord," she said, dipping into a small curtsy. "I was sorry that you couldn't join us on our visit to the royal menagerie."

Lord Eddings returned her greeting with a slight bow. "As was I. I heard a good time was had by all."

"Castlefield," Ellen said, not bothering to curtsy. His family was already familiar with their rivalry and wouldn't take it as an insult.

"It is so good to have you here, Ellen. It's been far too long."

Before she realized his intent, he'd taken hold of her hand and raised it. He looked down at her bare hand in his own gloveless one before looking up again to meet her gaze. He lifted a brow in silent question.

It took a great deal of effort to not snatch her hand away but instead wait for him to kiss the air above her wrist.

The duchess gave her head a shake. "Stop tormenting the girl, Charles. She's had a long journey with no stops, I'd imagine, to arrive so early. She's in no mood for your antics."

"Of course, Mother," he said. But Ellen could tell by the slight twinkle in his eyes that he was far from sorry.

A footman entered then, saving her from having to respond to Castlefield's teasing. But as Ellen took a seat and watched Her Grace pour the tea, she couldn't help glancing at where Castlefield sat opposite her, sprawled in an armchair.

For the first time in their acquaintance, she found herself remarking on just how attractive he was. Not just acknowledging the fact but noticing his looks in a way a woman would a man to whom she was attracted. She blamed that fact on their conversations leading up to this visit. It was almost impossible not to see him as a very desirable man. One who, if he was to be believed, wanted to pay court to her.

He could try, of course, but he wouldn't be the first man to attempt to take advantage of her widowed status.

She found her spirits lifting and told herself it was because she was looking forward to capturing another frog and placing it in his bed at his first misstep. It was a childish impulse, but it brought a smile to her face.

CHAPTER 7

S HE'D ONLY JUST ARRIVED, but Ellen could already feel her concerns starting to fade away. As she took in all the animated faces around the dining room table that evening, the conversation washing over her, she realized she was happy. She'd missed this, being with her second family. It had been far too many years since they'd spent the summer together, and nostalgia had her firmly in its grip.

She hadn't forgotten her concern with regard to her brother and his new bride and the current line of inquiry they were pursuing. But it wasn't as though Brantford hadn't been in some difficult situations before. She knew he could handle himself and that he would protect Rose with his life. Not that it would come to that, of course. It was impossible to imagine a situation in which her brother wouldn't triumph.

After the meal was over, the dowager duchess

approached her and gave her a quick embrace. "I'm so glad you decided to visit. Alas, I am no longer a young woman, so I will be retiring for the night. In case I need to say it, please treat this as your home while you are here. You are free to go anywhere."

Ellen smiled at the older woman, remembering just how fond she'd always been of Castlefield's mother. "I wanted to visit the gardens before turning in. I find I'm more than a little fatigued myself. I barely slept at all last night in anticipation of being here again."

She watched as the duchess swept from the room, Jane and her husband following. Jane had already told her they liked to look in on their children in the evening and spend a little time with them before they went to sleep.

As she headed out to the gardens, Ellen couldn't help but wonder where Castlefield had gone. She'd turned to take her leave of him after bidding his mother good night and realized he'd already left the dining room.

The sun had set, and moonlight cast an other-worldly glow on the lush green of the manicured shrubs. She made her way down the main path, her thoughts drifting to past summers when she and Castlefield used to chase each other, playing hide-and-seek among the benches and plants. Of course, that was before Brantford had grown into someone Castlefield had deemed interesting. It was the three of them for some time, then four when Jane, who was four years her and Castlefield's junior, was old enough to join them. Ellen still remembered the day Castlefield had told her he was too old to play with girls. That had brought about the beginning of their rivalry.

Out of habit, she turned right and made her way to the rose garden, which had always been her favorite place to visit whenever she stayed there. She took in a deep breath of the perfumed air as she walked under the arbor to the secluded haven, halting for a moment when she realized Castlefield was standing amid the red blooms. He looked up at her and smiled as though they'd arranged this meeting.

"I thought you'd escaped for the evening," she said, ignoring the anticipation that surged through her in that moment. She certainly wasn't happy to be alone with the man.

"I thought I'd intercept your attempt at mischief. I haven't forgotten your love of frogs, and I know all too well just how prevalent they are in the pond here."

Ellen couldn't help it, she laughed aloud at being caught. She'd been of two minds as to whether to wait until he annoyed her first before leaving a surprise for him in his bed or going ahead and having her fun now. She'd decided to leave the decision to fate, planning to stroll past the pond that resided just beyond the rose garden. If a frog happened to be in sight without her looking for one, she'd have taken it as a sign to proceed. She'd never admit to him, however, that he knew her so well.

"Should we be alone out here? I wouldn't want you to accuse me of trying to trap you into marriage."

"My family would like nothing better than to see that happen. But you needn't worry that they'd force the issue."

His casual admission that his mother and sister were hoping for a match didn't sit well with her. In fact, she felt slightly uncomfortable. As one, they turned in the direction of the pond and walked in silence.

It was Castlefield who broke the silence. "I received word from your brother this afternoon."

Ellen tried to appear nonchalant when she replied. "What did he say? Are he and Rose well?"

He stopped and waited for her to turn and look at him. "You're worried about them."

She lifted one shoulder in a casual shrug. "I'm always worried about my brother. It's my job as his older sister."

"You're only two years older than him, and stop trying to avoid the subject. They'd led me to believe they were on their wedding trip to his estate, but his letter seems to indicate otherwise."

Ellen debated lying, but in the end decided to tell him as much as she could. He wouldn't betray any information about Brantford's movements, and since her brother wasn't on a mission that had anything to do with the Crown or the war with France, she imagined he'd tell Castlefield about it once the matter was settled. Otherwise Brantford wouldn't have told his friend anything that would lead Castlefield to suspect he and Rose weren't at his estate.

"You've no doubt heard about the scandal surrounding his new wife."

Castlefield nodded. "Her father confessed to treason."

"Yes, well Rose is convinced her father is innocent. And Brantford believes Lord Worthington might have confessed to the crime to prevent any harm from coming to his wife and daughter."

"I see," Castlefield said, his tone neutral.

To his credit, he didn't ask for any further information about Rose's father, which served to improve her opinion of him. Not that she'd thought him one to engage in idle gossip, and certainly not about the wife of his closest friend, but he was human. It was only natural to wonder about the details even if that curiosity didn't spring from maliciousness.

They started again along the path, neither speaking for almost a full minute. Ellen waited for him to say something, but it became clear he wasn't going to volunteer any further information about her brother's letter.

She wanted to demand he hand over the correspondence he'd received. There might be a message hidden between the lines that Castlefield wouldn't pick up on. Instead, keeping her tone even, she asked, "Can you share what the letter said?"

"I can do better than that. You can read it for yourself." With a smile, he reached into his coat pocket and pulled out a folded sheet of paper.

She couldn't hold back a small huff of annoyance as she took the page. His fingers were bare, as were hers, so she took great care to avoid touching him.

"You could have just handed me the letter at the start of this conversation if you were going to allow me to read it."

"I find that I quite like making you beg."

Her eyes narrowed. "I never beg."

"Not yet, perhaps, but one day soon you will."

Shrugging off the thrill that went through her at the intimate tone of his voice—telling herself she was merely looking forward to proving him wrong—she unfolded the paper. The moon provided enough light that she was able to read it without too much difficulty.

Castlefield,

I was surprised to receive Ellen's note informing me she'd decided to renew our family tradition and spend the rest of the summer in Sussex. I feel it prudent to warn you that she carries a dagger for her personal protection and knows well how to use it, so watch your back.

Ellen couldn't hold back her smile of amusement as she imagined how Castlefield would have received that bit of news. She wondered how long it would take him to ask her about it. But it was more likely he thought Lucien was joking.

I am writing to you because she didn't say when she was planning to arrive and I didn't want to chance my missive going astray. I know she's concerned, so please convey to her the news that Rose and I have met with a measure of success. We are on our way to London now to see to matters there.

If it's not too forward, my wife has been through a great deal of stress throughout this whole ordeal. Originally I'd planned to return to our estate and spend the rest of the summer there in solitude. But I believe it would do her good to be in the company of family and friends. She and Ellen have grown close despite the shortness of their acquaintance.

Our families have never stood on ceremony, and I know your mother always welcomed us with open arms. Unless I hear otherwise, you should expect a visit in a week or two.

—Brantford

Ellen's relief was so profound she didn't care that

she was grinning like a fool. Without coming out and saying so directly, her brother was telling her they'd found the proof they were searching for. If they were on their way back to London, that meant he was hoping to present that proof and see to the release of Rose's father. Brantford's wife must be beyond relieved that this dark chapter of her family's lives would soon be over.

And Lucien and Rose would be joining them here within the fortnight.

"One day I'll get the full story out of Brantford, but I'm glad things appear to have worked out for my friend and his new countess."

"As am I. I was concerned about how Rose was handling this situation."

For a moment Castlefield seemed to weigh his words before asking, "Did she wed him solely to gain his assistance in proving her father's innocence?"

Ellen gave her head a firm shake. "Absolutely not. She cares for him a great deal. In fact, I believe she loves him. And he cares about her as well or he never would have married her. Heaven knows, he's more than capable of handling situations like the one in which her family found themselves. The fact that he married her to keep her safe speaks volumes about the depth of his feelings for her."

Her words seemed to have set his mind at ease. "I thought as much, but Brantford would hardly be the first man in existence to care for his wife more than she does for him. I'm glad to hear that isn't the case here."

"No, it isn't. There's nothing worse than unrequited love, especially when one discovers that the object of that love is undeserving of it."

Somehow she kept from wincing when she realized what she'd just admitted. She glanced up at Castlefield and was relieved to see he wasn't looking at her with pity. In fact, he wasn't looking at her at all but at the path ahead. She didn't miss the way his jaw had tensed.

For one horror-filled moment, she wondered if Brantford had shared with this man the details of her marriage. But no, surely her brother wouldn't have betrayed her confidence. He was used to keeping all manner of secrets in the work he did for the government. He'd never share what she'd revealed to him.

She shook off the thought. For all she knew, Castlefield had received his own disappointments in the field of love, perhaps even as a direct result of the rumors she'd spread about him. Rumors that had seemed innocent at the time. Yes, they'd served to give him the reputation of the unsuitable duke, but she knew there were more than a few women who would be drawn to his dangerous reputation.

Her new line of thought was almost more distressing than the previous one, and she realized the last thing she wanted to do was think about Castlefield's love affairs.

He was no longer walking, and she didn't notice until he touched her elbow. She stopped and turned to face him, surprised to see his brow wrinkled with concern.

"What is it?" she asked when he didn't speak right away.

"I'd like to ask you a favor."

A younger version of herself would have replied with a simple "anything." But she was older and wiser now. "What is it?"

"I'd like to call for a truce in the hostilities between us."

Ellen almost laughed at the ridiculousness of that request. "I would hardly call our current interaction hostile."

"No," he said with a slight frown. "Of course not. It was a turn of phrase. I meant that I want us to be friends again."

Her traitorous heart felt odd sitting in her chest, and she couldn't say why. She told herself it was because being here—even though it had been less than a day—had brought up so many happy memories and she was finding that she missed her friendship with Castlefield.

Aiming for a levity she was far from feeling, she said, "Surely you're not so frightened of a little frog. You must have spotted a snake and are worried I'll see it as well."

One corner of his mouth lifted in amusement.

"I've missed you, Ellen. I'm glad you decided to accept my sister's invitation."

"As am I," she said, ignoring the shimmer of moonlight in Castlefield's dark hair and the way shadows accented the planes of his face. He was an attractive man, and in that moment she was aware of him in a way that made her feel more than a little uncomfortable. It was a good thing she was no longer a maiden given to flights of romantic fantasy, or she'd be in danger of conjuring all manner of nonsense surrounding this moonlit stroll. "But that doesn't mean you shouldn't check your bed before going to sleep tonight."

CHAPTER 8

*I*T TOOK ELLEN one week to realize she was behaving irrationally.

For the most part she spent that time with Jane and, on occasion, the children. She went for long walks, and she even managed to find a quiet room in which to perform the skills her brother had taught her so that they remained sharp. She clung to that activity now more than ever to remind herself she was still in control.

Her awareness of her childhood nemesis made her wonder if she was attracted to him and led her to avoid him whenever possible. She told herself she wasn't hiding from him but acting in a logical fashion. No good could come from moonlit strolls through a fragrant garden when one was feeling sentimental about the past. She had no reason to believe Castlefield would be waiting for her again in the rose garden, but it wasn't a chance she wanted to take.

When she woke up that morning, however, she realized she'd been acting the coward.

She hadn't been able to avoid him entirely, of course, since they were both at his estate. And thus far he hadn't done anything to warrant her leaving any surprises for him in his bed. She was of two minds about that. On the one hand, it would be nice to get through this visit without any negativity. But if he was sincere about wanting to woo her, she was uncomfortable with the idea of a cessation of hostilities between them.

Whatever his real motives, it became clearer as each day passed that he wasn't planning to put too much effort into that endeavor. Surely if he was intent on courting her, he would go out of his way to seek her company. Since they'd last spoken, she'd only seen him during the evening meals when his family was also present.

She most certainly wasn't disappointed by that fact.

From those dinner conversations, it became clear he was spending part of his days entertaining his nephew and niece. The revelation of that fact baffled her at first, but then she began to wonder if he was choosing to spend time there because of their young nanny.

She told herself it was only curiosity that had her

visiting the nursery that afternoon. The room was situated on the second floor of the house, facing the back gardens. Ellen approached the open doorway and raised one hand to tap lightly on the doorframe, but she stopped short when she took in the scene before her. She refused to acknowledge the odd fluttering sensation in her chest.

Henry had his head bent over a task at a low table while his nurse supervised from a seat next to him. But what drew her attention was the way Castlefield held his young niece against his chest and smiled down at her. When he spoke to Hope, it was in what could only be called a singsong voice.

He would be a good father. Hard on the heels of that discovery was her certainty that she didn't want to see him cooing over a baby he'd had with another woman. It was unfair that men could put off matrimony and have no concerns about being able to father children while, at thirty-two, she could well be past the age of bearing her own.

She had to look away from Castlefield to collect her wayward emotions. She'd already decided she would never wed again, so it didn't matter whether she was capable of having children.

After giving herself a moment, Ellen tapped lightly against the doorframe and stepped into the spacious room. She expected Castlefield to act as though she hadn't witnessed him doing something most men would consider embarrassing. Instead, one corner of his mouth lifted in a lopsided smile. It reminded her so much of the young boy with whom she'd once been friends. To her surprise, he continued speaking to Hope in that same lilting tone.

Ignoring the way it unsettled her to watch him playing with his young niece, she did her best to keep her voice even. "When I learned that you liked to visit the nursery, I was convinced Jane was having one over on me."

He gave her an enigmatic look she couldn't decipher. "It's no secret I've always had a close relationship with my family, and it's almost impossible to resist the exuberance of youth. Even if Henry and Hope do make me feel old."

"That's because you are old, Uncle Charles."

Ellen laughed, watching as Henry looked to his nurse. Both had risen to their feet when she made her presence known.

The young woman stood with her arms crossed, a frown creasing her brow. "What have I told you about insulting your elders, young man?"

"I'm sorry," Henry said. But it was clear from the twinkle in his eyes before he looked away that he was far from being repentant.

"It appears that your nephew has inherited your penchant for mischief," Ellen said, her tone dry.

She couldn't hold back her smile at the way Castlefield shook his head, an expression of mock dismay on his face. "And the world continues to turn."

"So it does."

Castlefield's gaze softened, and she found it almost impossible to look away. She disliked this man standing before her, so why was her heart beginning to soften just because he was holding a young child in his arms? One who appeared to have just fallen asleep.

"It seems that Hope finds your company less than scintillating." She wanted to add something about whether that was a problem he had with all women, but she was conscious of the other woman in the room with them. The children's nurse was fussing over Henry, but Ellen could tell she was very interested in the conversation she was having with Castlefield. She couldn't help but remember how her husband had dallied with most of the younger women on their household staff and found herself wondering, not for the first time, if there was anything between the nurse and Castlefield. The thought bothered her more than it should.

"I'll admit I've taken to coming up here about this time every day so I can spend a few minutes with my niece before she sleeps away the afternoon. She was little more than a babe the last time I saw her. I can scarce believe how much she's grown."

Castlefield handed the sleeping child to her nurse, who had materialized at his side when Ellen mentioned she'd fallen asleep. Ellen watched them carefully for any signs of familiarity. She was well acquainted with the blushing and averted gazes that had passed between her husband and many of the young maids in their household. But she saw nothing untoward about the way Castlefield and the children's nurse interacted.

She didn't realize Henry had moved until she felt a small hand sliding into hers. "Uncle Charles is taking me to the stables for my riding lesson."

He'd tried to lower his voice, but as was often the case with children, Henry's attempt to whisper fell far short of the mark. The nurse cast a fond smile his way before disappearing through another doorway with Hope.

"Can you come with us?" Henry asked.

Henry's question caught her off guard. She glanced at Castlefield, who lifted one shoulder in a casual shrug as if to say he'd had nothing to do with the spontaneous invitation. The man might not have had the opportunity to conspire with his nephew, but that didn't mean he wasn't going to take advantage of the opportunity with which he'd been presented.

Ellen didn't have the heart to deny Henry's request, even if her initial inclination was to continue avoiding the boy's uncle. But she reminded herself that she wasn't going to hide from him any longer. After all, she was more than up to the task of spending a few moments walking side by side with Castlefield.

"That sounds like a wonderful idea. It's a lovely afternoon, and I was thinking of going for a stroll."

Henry started to tug on her hand but stopped abruptly and gave her a sheepish smile. "Nurse says I must remember to be patient."

"I know how difficult that can be," Castlefield said. "But I have it on good authority that good things come to those who wait." There was something odd in the tone of his voice that unsettled Ellen. Especially when his eyes flitted from Henry's to meet hers again before he turned back to his nephew. "Or so I've been told. And if I can learn to be patient, I know you can as well."

Ellen refrained from comment. It would hardly set a good example, after all, to start needling Castlefield in front of an impressionable child.

They made their way from the nursery with Henry filling the silence that had settled between the two adults with stories about his riding lessons and how much he had improved since last year.

Henry kept his hand in hers the entire way, and Castlefield fell into step on the boy's other side.

A small part of her hoped Castlefield would take his leave at some point before they reached the stables. She could tell herself then that she was no longer hiding from him even while she avoided dealing with her confusing emotions. But if there was one thing she'd come to accept, it was that her life had never been easy.

Castlefield stayed with them the entire way, inter-jecting a comment only when Henry asked him a question. Ellen kept her gaze on the child, but she didn't miss the way Castlefield's body tensed slightly when they reached the stables.

"Smithers?" he called out.

Ellen turned to face him then, not bothering to hide her surprise. "He's still here?"

Castlefield nodded toward the back of the stables where a wiry older man had poked his head out from one of the stalls. He was much older than Ellen remembered, his hair almost entirely white now and his skin weathered from time spent in the sun. But he was definitely the same man who'd been in charge of the stables when her family used to visit.

"You're early," he said. "Wasn't expecting you for another half hour."

Ellen laughed—time hadn't mellowed the man one bit. "I can't believe you're still here. I thought you would have gotten tired of His Grace long before now."

Smithers had turned toward her, his head tilted to the side as he tried to place her. She could tell the moment he did by the way his blue eyes lit up.

"As I live and breathe, it's good to see you again, Miss Ellen. I wondered when you'd come to visit."

She saw Castlefield open his mouth to correct the man, but Ellen forestalled him with a quick tap on his arm. She didn't want to be reminded that she was now Dowager Viscountess Laughton. And it wasn't as though she wasn't used to being treated with such familiarity. Ellen had taken on many guises over the past two years when working for her brother, and she didn't mind the old stable master's lack of formality.

He'd gotten away with it when he first came to work for Castlefield's father because the man had no equal when it came to tending horses. He'd always known where to draw the line, however. And now she imagined he was almost a member of the family.

"Should we come back later?" Henry asked. It was clear from the expression on the young boy's face —a mixture of hope and dread—that he hadn't wanted to ask the question.

Smithers scowled in contemplation, making the boy wait just long enough to have Henry almost jumping out of his skin with anticipation, before smiling.

"I'm always happy to see you, Mr. Henry," he said. "You can help me saddle your mount before your riding lesson."

Henry took one step forward before turning back and giving Ellen a formal bow. She curtsied in return, a fond smile on her face as she watched him walk away with Smithers.

Castlefield turned and waited for her to fall in step beside him as he walked away from the stables. Her thoughts filled with memories of past summers when Smithers had overseen their own childhood outings.

Castlefield glanced at her as they made their way back to the house. "I haven't seen much of you over the past week."

If he was hoping to get her to admit she'd been avoiding him, he would be disappointed. "You've seen me every evening at dinner."

He halted before a large oak tree, one they'd both climbed many times during their youth. Ellen was tempted to keep walking, but she came to a stop as well.

"It's not nearly enough, Ellen. I was hoping we could regain our friendship at the very least."

And just like that, she realized it hadn't been the moonlight that led her to realize just how attractive she found Castlefield. His dark eyes seemed to bore right through her, and a sense of anticipation had her heart rate increasing. She'd never admit it to him though. She could scarce stand the fact she'd come to that disturbing realization.

A change of subject was in order. "Jane has been keeping me occupied. And when she's busy elsewhere, I've been going for walks. Reacquainting myself with the area."

"Of course," he said, leaning back against the oak.

"I assumed you'd be too busy to notice." It was a lie, but she hoped he'd be too much of a gentleman to contradict her. She was wrong.

"While I'm sure that's true, we both know you've been avoiding me."

Ellen crossed her arms, knowing the stance was a defensive one but not caring in that moment. "I don't want to have this conversation again."

His eyes narrowed the tiniest fraction, and she knew he wanted to press the matter. In the end, he lifted one shoulder in a casual shrug and began to walk back to the house. Ellen followed, determined to hold on to her poise.

"Jane and her family will be heading to Brighton soon," Castlefield said. "They're eager to take possession of their new estate. We're close to the sea here, but not close enough for her liking."

"I've always liked Brighton." Ellen would miss Castlefield's sister, but now that they'd repaired the breach in their friendship, she knew she'd see her again soon.

"I remember."

Ellen glanced at him and couldn't help wondering what he was thinking. "I find it a little worrying that she hasn't invited me to visit."

Castlefield glanced at her. "You must know that Jane is matchmaking. She doesn't want to see us separated so soon. But worry not, she'll ask you to join them before the summer is over."

She hadn't expected him to acknowledge his sister's efforts bring the two of them together. "I see."

He chuckled at her simple reply. "You never used

to be so closed off. What happened to the carefree girl who wouldn't have thought twice about telling me what she really thought of that sentiment?"

"She got married."

She must not have done a good job at keeping all hint of emotion from her voice, for Castlefield stopped walking and turned to face her again. She expected to see pity in his eyes and steeled herself when she met his gaze. Instead, she saw a hint of anger.

"Yes, she did. And I blame myself for that."

Ellen dropped all pretense of indifference. "I'm not sure I understand."

"Do you remember that summer when your brother and I had just returned from school? It was his first year, and I stayed with your family for a few days before continuing here."

She remembered it well. She'd wanted her brother to be the first person, aside from her parents, to learn she'd accepted Laughton's proposal. She'd been so excited to share the news she hadn't even cared that Castlefield was present when she'd told Brantford.

"I do. I remember Lucien's less than enthusiastic reception to the news, but I'd expected that. He's always been one to hide his emotions. It was your reaction that hurt. We'd been friends once, and I thought you'd be happy for me."

Instead, he'd said something about Laughton only wanting her for her name and connections. Told her it

86

wasn't possible the man who'd been wooing her so diligently actually cared for her, let alone loved her. The seeds of her hatred for this man had been sown on that day, made only worse when she discovered he'd been correct.

His jaw tightened, and she got the distinct impression he was wrestling with what to say. She didn't have to wait long before he replied.

"How could I be happy? Something fundamental shifted within me that day. I don't know why, but when you came outside to greet your brother, all smiles and dressed in blue, it was as though I was seeing you for the first time. I'd never seen you happier... or more beautiful." He gave his head a slight shake. "And every fiber of my being rebelled at the thought another man was responsible."

Ellen examined his face, certain he must be lying, but could see no signs of deception. Still, she couldn't make herself believe what he seemed to be saying. "No."

He stepped closer but didn't reach for her, keeping his hands clasped behind his back. "Yes, Ellen. I realized in that moment that I cared for you as far more than a friend. That I wanted you to be mine. And almost as soon as I'd come to that realization, I knew I'd lost you forever. That my stupid need to prove my family wrong—that we'd never be anything more than childhood friends—had led me to push you away and now it was too late. They'd been correct all along, seeing something in our friendship that I'd been too young to see, let alone acknowledge."

Ellen turned away from him. This couldn't be happening. "You never said a word."

"Oh, I believe I said plenty."

She whirled around to face him again. "About Laughton, yes. But nothing concrete. Did you know he was such a monster?"

The sadness in his eyes almost tore her heart in two. "No. I'd heard small rumblings about him being selfish, but hell, the same could be said of me. I never imagined—"

Ellen raised a hand to stop him from continuing. "Don't. If you have intimate details about my marriage, I don't want to know."

"Your brother didn't tell me anything. But I learned soon enough how he was with other women. And I had to trust that Brantford would keep you safe."

He had. Her brother had taught her how to defend herself against the superior strength of a man. Taught her how to use a dagger, one that she kept strapped to her thigh to this day. But not before her husband had shown his true colors.

"I should have told you how I felt instead of lashing out because of my jealousy."

Several emotions threatened to overtake her. The first was regret and anger, but not at Castlefield. She was angry with herself. At the naive, silly girl she'd once been.

"It wouldn't have mattered. Laughton played his part well. I truly believed he loved me, and I loved him too much to have listened to you. You wouldn't have been able to sway me from my purpose. But you should know that I'm no longer the same foolish young woman. I won't be easily won with sweet words."

"I find that my tastes fall to women who know what they want." He leaned in closer, causing her breath to hitch when she saw the warmth in his eyes. "Tell me, Ellen, what it is you want when you're all alone in your room at night?"

She knew it would be unwise to answer, but no one had ever asked her that question before, and she found she wanted to tell him. Open herself to this man who had known her longer than even her own brother.

"I don't know if I have it in me to trust another man. But if I could, I'd want to be with someone who sees me for who I am. Not just as a trophy to be taken out and displayed on occasion."

Silence stretched between them for several long moments before Castlefield replied. "I see you."

Just like that, she was lost. In that moment she didn't care if he was telling her the truth. She hadn't ever acknowledged that desire to even herself, but being here was wreaking havoc on her defenses. She blamed it on the sentimentality caused by being in Sussex again. It didn't help that she'd been witness to many displays of affection between Jane and her husband.

And heaven help her, she was drawn to the man standing before her in a way she'd never imagined possible.

He reached for her hand and she allowed him to take it.

"We shouldn't do this." Her words came out in a breathless whisper.

"Can I kiss you, Ellen?"

She should deny his request. Tell him that nothing could happen between them and then return to the house alone. Instead, her gaze dipped to his mouth as she wondered what it would feel like to kiss a man who wasn't her now-dead husband.

"I'm going to take your silence as agreement."

CHAPTER 9

CASTLEFIELD FOUND HIMSELF staring into Ellen's exquisite eyes as her gaze met his. Her face was tilted up in invitation, her blue eyes wide and her breathing uneven. He waited a beat longer before moving, not wanting any doubt to remain about whether she wanted him to stop. When she didn't step away, he lowered his head.

Triumph surged within him when her lids began to lower. He closed his eyes and angled his head slightly, anticipation heavy in his veins.

In the next moment he was flat on his back, staring up at the cloudy sky.

Ellen stood a foot away, the expression on her face telling him she was just as surprised as he with how this moment had ended.

"I didn't mean… I don't know…" She gave her head a sharp shake and sighed. "Did I hurt you?"

He was powerless to stop the laugh that burst from him. He tried to rein in his amusement, but the look of indignation on Ellen's face set him off again. He should have known nothing would be easy with her.

She towered over him, frowning, her arms crossed beneath the tempting display of her attributes. Her lips twitched with the telltale sign that she was trying to hold back her own amusement.

He rose to his feet, another chuckle escaping.

"I really must apologize," she said. "I don't know what came over me."

From the haunted look that flickered in her eyes, he knew exactly what had come over her. Memories of Laughton and everything he must have done to her before she'd learned how to toss a grown man onto his back with seemingly little effort.

"No harm done. As you well know, I've taken more than my share of tumbles over the years."

He was relieved when the tension broke and the corners of her mouth lifted in a genuine smile. "Did you and my brother ever decide who was the better horseman?"

"I am, of course. Although if you ask him, he'll no doubt tell you I don't know what I'm talking about."

She looked away and he waited. When she met his gaze again, she didn't conceal her unhappiness. "I fear I'm not very good at this. You should consider moving on to someone better worth your time and effort. Someone younger."

With a slow, careful movement, he reached for her hand. He half expected to find himself on his back again, but she accepted his touch. They were both wearing gloves, and he wondered briefly if she'd have allowed the small intimacy if that weren't the case.

"I've waited this long, I can wait a little longer."

Her head tilted to the side, her eyes seeming to bore right through him. "At times you almost have me believing the nonsense you're spouting is true."

"It is, and one of these days you're going to believe me."

After giving her hand a squeeze, he released it. He couldn't help adding, "Next time, I'll allow you to initiate the kiss. Perhaps then I won't have to worry that I'll be being flung about by you."

"You seem very confident that day will come."

"It will," he said. It had to.

CHAPTER 10

*E*LLEN DIDN'T COME DOWN for dinner that evening, and Castlefield knew he was to blame. He'd spoken too soon, revealed too much of his feelings. And even worse, stirred up memories about her now-deceased husband when he'd tried to kiss her. But he'd spent far too many years filled with regret for not speaking out when he had the opportunity. After Laughton's death, he knew Ellen wouldn't mourn her husband. Still, knowing he couldn't rush her, he'd waited for the appropriate amount of time to pass.

He'd gone over his options many times in his head and knew there would never be a good time to tell her it had been many years since he realized he cared for her as more than a former childhood friend. So much more.

His past mistakes continued to haunt him. They'd

been inseparable all those summers when they were growing up. He'd been twelve when he first realized their parents were pushing them together, hoping to unite their two families. He'd thought it fine to have a girl as his best friend, but the idea of marrying her was so foreign and unwelcome, and he'd wanted nothing to do with their plans. But it wasn't until he'd spoken out against Ellen's betrothed, blind jealousy causing him to be less than kind about the man with whom Ellen had fallen in love, that she'd grown to hate him.

He wouldn't allow that to happen again now that they were both older and wiser. Even if Ellen could never come to care for him in return, he was determined to tear down the barriers that lay between them. The task wasn't an easy one, but if he must, he'd accept Ellen as nothing more than a good friend again.

He ignored the stab of pain caused by the thought of watching from afar as she fell in love with another man. But right now it was his time—their time—and if she'd allow it, he was going to show her what it really meant to have a man love her the way she deserved.

After watching her walk away from him the day before, he decided not to press his luck this morning. Normally he ate early before anyone else had risen and went for a ride, enjoying the peaceful start to his day. He would return about an hour later and head into his study to look over the paperwork that always seemed to multiply overnight.

It was only to be expected since his title came with many estates, and so he generally devoted the rest of the morning to answering correspondence from the stewards at his various estates, reading through their suggestions for improvements and weighing them against the income each estate brought in. On those days that a set of accounts waited for him, he knew he was in for a tedious afternoon as well. Still, the work would only pile up if he ignored it, and so he made it a habit to tackle matters as they came up.

But after Ellen's absence over dinner the evening before, he considered avoiding the correspondence that still remained on his desk from the previous day and, instead, waiting for her in the breakfast room. From what Jane had told him, they usually spent some time together after breakfast, and his sister's presence would ensure there'd be no awkward silences. But he couldn't shake his worry that pressing Ellen now might cause her to return to London.

And so after returning from his early morning ride, he made his way to his study. As he lowered himself into the chair at his desk, he reached for the letter that had arrived the previous day. He didn't need to read it again. It was a few lines from Brantford telling Castlefield that he and his new wife would be arriving sometime this afternoon. He could always use the news as an excuse to talk to Ellen at breakfast.

He gave his head a shake and pushed the short note off to the side of his desk. Much as he wanted to force the issue of their relationship, he'd leave Ellen to her peaceful morning routine. He'd see her later, after her brother and sister-in-law arrived. She wouldn't be hiding in her room again this evening, so now was the time to plan his next move.

CHAPTER 11

*E*LLEN HAD ALMOST given up hope of seeing her brother and his new wife in Sussex. A full week had passed since he'd sent that note to Castlefield, and they'd had no further word.

Her initial instinct after her disastrous near kiss with Castlefield yesterday was to ask for a carriage to be readied so she could return to London. She resisted the impulse and instead pleaded a headache and retired to her room for the rest of the day. She liked to think she was no longer that impulsive young woman of twenty who'd thought herself about to wed the man of her dreams, but in truth she wasn't immune to making rash decisions she'd come to regret later. At least now she was mature enough to know she needed to wait at least a day for her emotions to settle before deciding on a course of action.

She couldn't deny that as each day passed without

another letter, her worry that something had gone wrong with Brantford and his wife grew. Perhaps he hadn't been able to save Rose's father from the hangman's noose after all. The note he'd sent Castlefield seemed to indicate otherwise, but it might not matter that the man wasn't, in fact, guilty. He'd confessed to treason to protect the lives of his wife and daughter. That might not be something he could retract even with Brantford's influence.

As the new day dawned, Ellen realized she didn't want to leave. She told herself it was because she didn't want to be separated from Jane again so soon, but the truth was far more disturbing.

After Castlefield had confessed he felt a romantic interest in her all those years ago, her mind had blanked with shock and she'd needed to get away. But now that she'd had the opportunity to ruminate on the matter, she couldn't deny she was intrigued. At the very least, his actions were a puzzle she longed to unravel.

He'd told her at the masquerade that he meant to court her, and she'd thought he was playing another game with her. Was it possible he cared for her in truth? Or did he just want her to believe that so he could gain the upper hand in the war that had developed between them in their adult years?

Even though her husband had been dead for two years, Ellen was aware that he still influenced her thoughts and actions. She didn't know if a day would ever come when she'd be able to take someone's word at face value. She couldn't even say whether she wanted that day to come. Her unshakable belief in the motives of others had certainly done her no favors in the past.

Still, she knew she couldn't run away from what was happening between her and Castlefield. Not until she discovered the truth behind his words.

Her decision to stay made, Ellen headed downstairs to the breakfast room. Normally he didn't join them for the morning meal, so she didn't expect she'd have to deal with him first thing. She ignored the slight twinge of disappointment that today was no different.

She greeted Jane, Lord Eddings, and the dowager duchess and sat down at the table. She couldn't help but wonder what the day would hold. For the first time in years, the future seemed filled with possibilities.

It was midday before she saw Castlefield again. She couldn't decide whether he was playing a game of cat and mouse with her or if he was giving her the space he no doubt thought she needed after his confession the day before. But whichever was true, she was determined to set aside her doubts when he joined her in the library.

She had chosen a novel and was curled up in a comfortable armchair next to a window that overlooked a smaller side garden. Jane had gone up to the nursery to spend time with her children, and Ellen had taken to spending that time in the library.

She looked up when she sensed movement by the doorway and was surprised to find Castlefield standing there. The stiff set of his shoulders told her he wasn't sure of his reception. Ellen was happy to set aside the book, which hadn't captured her interest, and gave Castlefield a guarded smile. She could almost see the tension lift from him. Certainly his own smile became warm instead of cautious.

"If you're in search of a book, I can recommend one you shouldn't read," she said with an exaggerated scowl at the thick volume she'd set aside.

The sound of Castlefield's laugh lifted her spirits. "I'm here to inform you that we have two guests arriving."

She rose to her feet, almost afraid he was teasing her again. "Brantford is here?"

"His carriage is pulling up in front of the house even as we speak." He hesitated for a moment before continuing. "I may have received a note yesterday informing me of his impending arrival. I hope you'll forgive me for keeping that knowledge to myself, but I wanted to surprise you."

She couldn't find it within herself to be even a little annoyed as a mixture of relief and happiness swept over her. Everything must have worked out as her brother and sister-in-law had hoped. She'd only known Rose a short while before the two wed, but in that time she'd seen just how fiercely loyal the woman was. Rose never would have left her father's side if he was still sentenced to be hanged. Which could only mean her brother had succeeded in proving Lord Worthington innocent of the crime of treason.

Castlefield stepped aside, and she thanked him as she moved into the hallway. Together, they made their way to the front of the house.

"I should be angry with you for keeping Brantford's letter from me, but I'm just so relieved."

A corner of his mouth lifted. "Your smile is worth any ire I might have risked."

Ellen couldn't stop the small laugh that escaped her. For some reason it no longer bothered her that Castlefield seemed to have decided it was safe to proceed with his plan to court her. She was more than equal to the task of holding her own against him. In fact, she found herself looking forward to the challenge.

Voices led them to the front drawing room, which was filled with people. Jane and the dowager duchess were absent, but Lord Eddings was deep in conversation with Brantford and Rose. A footman hovered in the hallway, no doubt awaiting further instructions.

What caught Ellen's attention as she stood in the doorway was the fond smile on her brother's face as he gazed at his wife. It was plain to see she'd just said something that amused him. Ellen had known he cared for Rose when he'd asked her to watch over the young woman earlier this year. She'd even teased him about his feelings before he declared his intention to wed her. He'd told her that he was marrying Rose for the sole purpose of keeping her safe, but Ellen had known he harbored feelings for the young woman. Despite that, she was shocked her brother was so open with his emotions.

She'd rarely seen even a hint of warmth in his expression over the past several years. Wry humor, yes, but never an open display of affection. Not since he was a boy, before the weight of expectation their father had placed squarely on his young shoulders had turned him into a remote stranger.

It struck her that she was no longer looking at the Earl of Brantford as the world saw him—the man everyone had taken to calling the unaffected earl—but at her brother, Lucien. Until that moment, she hadn't realized just how much she'd missed him.

The revelation left her with the odd sensation that somehow the world had shifted. Her brother was a master at reining in his emotions, leaving others to guess what he was thinking or feeling. And since he had a certain quality that had everyone wanting to gain his approval, that meant they worked all the harder for the smallest sign that Brantford liked them. She couldn't remember the last time she'd seen him so open.

It wasn't just that he was smiling down at Rose that made her chest feel tight. The expression on her brother's face made it clear to anyone who looked at them that Brantford loved his wife. If anyone harbored any doubts as to that fact, those doubts would be banished the moment they saw the two of them together.

Ellen shook off her shock and moved into the room to greet the new arrivals. "When we didn't receive any news, I despaired we'd see the two of you here this summer."

She gave Rose a quick hug, whispering, "How did everything go?" She'd have to wait to learn all the details, but she hoped to hear confirmation that their mission had gone well.

Rose's smile was answer enough. "I'll tell you everything later."

A corresponding smile spread across Ellen's face. She nodded, squeezing Rose's hands before turning to face her brother.

"Ellen," he said by way of greeting. But there was a twinkle in his eyes she hadn't seen in years. Oh, how she'd missed her mischievous younger brother.

"I'm so happy you've joined us, Lucien."

Her brother raised a brow at her use of his given name. She'd taken to calling him by his title after he inherited, telling him that she missed the carefree youth he'd once been. His mouth twitched, and he gave her an exaggerated bow. The way he looked at her though, with a genuine warmth she hadn't seen in years, told her that he understood the reason behind her uncharacteristic use of his Christian name. And if she wasn't mistaken, it pleased him.

Oh yes, Rose had performed a true miracle in the short time she'd been in her brother's life.

Rose was a striking young woman, her dark chestnut-colored hair contrasting with her brother's fair coloring. But as well as beauty, her new sister-in-law also had charm, wit, and an intelligence that made her a perfect match for Brantford.

Ellen watched as the young woman turned that charm on Castlefield now.

"My husband has promised me a proper wedding trip at a later date, but neither of us could ignore the lure of friends and family. Thank you for allowing us to stay."

Ellen couldn't help but contrast the woman before her now with the one who'd been so hurt when everyone she'd considered a friend deserted her after her father confessed to treason. Brantford had been wise to bring her to Sussex. Ellen had only known Rose a short time before she married her brother, but in that time she already considered her a friend. She had no doubt Rose and Jane would soon become friends as well. Given how many of the women Rose had known deserted her when scandal touched her family, Ellen was eager to see that friendship develop.

As though thinking about her friend conjured her presence, Jane swept into the room and moved to her husband's side.

"Someone just told me we have guests." She made a deep curtsy before Brantford, her eyes glinting with amusement as she said, "My lord. I am so happy you decided to grace us with your presence."

To everyone but his wife's shock, Brantford laughed. Ellen couldn't believe this was the same Earl of Brantford who had left London scarcely a month before. She hadn't heard him laugh in years.

His voice was devoid of humor when he returned her greeting with a formal bow of his own. "Thank you for the invitation. Please allow me the honor of introducing my wife, the Countess of Brantford."

A dimple appeared in Jane's cheek as she curtsied again. "Your husband knows he is always welcome here. And I must say I am very happy to make your acquaintance, my lady."

Rose inclined her head. "Please call me Rose. I hope we can become friends, considering how close you all are."

Lord Eddings added, "I never thought I'd see the day Brantford would wed. But seeing the two of you together, I'm happy to find I was wrong. There are few things in life more rewarding than a happy marriage."

Lord Eddings glanced at his wife, and Ellen saw that his statement had pleased Jane.

Castlefield gave his head an exaggerated shake. "He's just pleased he won our wager. I probably shouldn't admit this, but Eddings and I had money on who would win your hand. He always maintained that if you did wed—something neither of us was sure would ever happen—it would be for love. I, on the other hand, was foolish enough to maintain you'd settle for a practical union. Someone who wouldn't even come close to touching your heart."

Brantford raised a brow at that. He and Castlefield had known each other long enough that her brother didn't have to speak, that motion alone conveying what he was thinking.

Castlefield let out a small chuckle. "Yes, I do believe I've finally learned never to anticipate your actions."

There was a round of laughter at the lighthearted chagrin in Castlefield's voice, but Ellen couldn't help but agree with him. Despite knowing that her brother had feelings for his wife and rejoicing when they'd wed, it was more than a little unsettling to see evidence that they actually loved one another.

She couldn't help thinking about her own unhappy marriage, but she quickly squashed the memories of her disappointment with her own union. Two happy couples, although rare, did not change the fact that most of the members of society married only for practical reasons.

"I'm surprised the duchess isn't here," Ellen said, seeking to change the subject from that of love in marriage. "I thought perhaps she might be in the nursery with you, Jane. Much as I know she wouldn't want to miss my brother's arrival, she will be more disappointed she wasn't here to meet Rose."

She could feel the weight of Castlefield's gaze on her but ignored him. She didn't want to risk meeting his eyes, which she attributed to the fact that unlike the other two couples in the room, there would never be any love between them. And while she didn't expect nor want that for herself at this stage of her life, she didn't need the reminder that her life was in some way lacking.

It wasn't Jane but Castlefield who replied. "Mother decided to pay a call on one of the neighbors. She'll be unhappy with me that I didn't tell her guests were arriving today, but I didn't want to ruin the surprise for Ellen."

Jane gave a small shrug. "I'm sure her joy at having the two of you here will overshadow her annoyance with my brother. I know she's eager to meet Brantford's wife." She turned to Rose, adding, "She's always considered him an honorary son."

Rose lifted a hand to her breast, her mouth turning down the smallest amount. "Should I be concerned?"

Brantford took her hand and placed a kiss on its back. "She will be just as enchanted by you as I am."

"Especially if she sees the two of you carrying on like that." Castlefield's wry comment had everyone laughing again.

"Never mind my brother," Jane said, glancing from Castlefield to Ellen. "He'll understand one day."

Ellen made it a point to look away. More than anything, she hated being the subject of gossip. The very last thing she wanted was for speculation to arise about her and Castlefield becoming a match. It was bad enough that Jane and her mother were hoping for that very outcome. She didn't want Rose or her brother adding their voices to the chorus.

Jane turned to Rose and continued. "We had the staff ready the green bedroom for your arrival when we received your fist missive stating your intention to visit. It's the same room Brantford used whenever their family visited."

Brantford inclined his head in acknowledgment, but his attempt to return to his more serious demeanor was foiled by Rose, who gave her husband an arch look before saying, "You're going to have to tell me what my husband was like as a boy. He would have me believe he's always been the same no-nonsense person he is today, but I find that impossible to believe."

Brantford let out a long-suffering sigh, but he couldn't quite manage his customary appearance of cool displeasure as he gazed at his wife.

Castlefield clapped him on the back. "That's our cue to leave, old man, before your sister skewers the two of us with her excellent memory."

Ellen couldn't hold back her laugh. "Which story

should I tell first? There are so many, it's going to take me a minute to decide."

"Right." Brantford dropped another quick kiss on the back of Rose's hand before turning to Ellen. "Try not to embarrass me too much." He turned to Jane's husband, saying, "Give us ten minutes before joining us?"

"Coward," Rose said to her departing husband's back.

Ellen tried to ignore the twinge of disappointment she felt as she watched her brother and Castlefield leave the room together. The situation brought back far too many memories of similar times when the two of them had gone off together, leaving her behind. Only this time they were expecting a third to join them, and it still wasn't her.

She refused to believe her disappointment had anything to do with the fact Castlefield had scarcely paid her any attention.

Shaking those thoughts from her mind, she turned to her new sister-in-law. "You've performed a miracle with my brother. He hardly seems the same man."

Jane shook her head. "I don't understand why everyone calls him by that ridiculous nickname. The unaffected earl. I've always found him to be very approachable."

"You are the exception then," Rose said as she settled into a chair, waiting a moment until Ellen and Jane took a seat on the settee. "I'm sure the fact that your families were so close and that you were practically raised together meant you got to see a side of him that few others have. I shouldn't admit this, but I'd despaired of ever getting him to look at me, let alone court me. And if you'd told me at the beginning of the season that we'd be wed within the year, I would have questioned your sanity."

"It's true," Ellen said with a sad shake of her head. "I always imagined that if my brother were to wed, it would be to someone as cold and emotionally distant as he. I thought the best that would come of such a union would be that his wife would tolerate my presence in their lives. Never did I imagine he'd come to care for someone as delightful as Rose. Someone who would truly become like a sister to me."

Jane cast a conspiratorial glance at Rose as she said, "Speaking of sisters…"

Rose's head snapped in Ellen's direction, her eyes widening. "What's this? Is there something between you and the duke? You must tell me everything."

Lord Eddings, who'd been watching on in silence, shook his head. "And with that, I must take my leave."

Jane made a moue of disappointment. "I didn't intend to chase you off."

"You didn't. I'm going to look in on the children before tracking down your brother. I must admit I'm intrigued by this new side to Brantford. I don't expect to see it outside his wife's presence, but one never knows."

Rose waited just long enough for Lord Eddings to leave the room before turning back to Ellen, her arms crossed and one brow raised in expectation.

Ellen had hoped not to have this conversation right away. "I fear Jane is engaging in a bout of wishful thinking. She's mistaken the truce between her brother and me as something more."

Her words only served to intrigue Rose. "Truce? Now this I have to hear. Last I heard, you were responsible for the rumors about Lord Castlefield being the unsuitable duke. Has that changed?"

Jane gasped. "That was you?"

Ellen was torn between laughter and guilt. "It seemed like a good idea at the time. He was so hateful to me."

Jane's brows drew together in a frown. "Not always. I was too young to remember, but Mother says the two of you were once very close."

Ellen lifted one shoulder in what she hoped was a casual gesture. "Yes, but that ended when we were still quite young. When he realized he infinitely preferred the friendship of men and could no longer be bothered with silly girls."

"He didn't actually say that to you?" Jane shook her head. "That doesn't sound at all like my brother."

"I wouldn't make up something like that." Ellen remembered how much it had hurt to hear those words.

"That sounds dreadful," Rose said. "But I'm not

surprised. Boys tend to reach a stage when they want nothing to do with girls. Then they reverse course and can think of little else a few years later."

"I think that might have been Mother's fault," Jane said. "She was pushing for a marriage between you two."

Ellen raised a brow as she gazed at her friend. "Well, I know it. In fact, it seems that you've taken up the habit as well."

Rose was almost bouncing in her seat. "Details please."

Ellen shook her head. "Pay it no mind. There is nothing romantic between His Grace and me."

"Well, it has been some time since you arrived, and I've yet to hear my brother complain you've left a snake in his bed, so you can't hate him that much."

Rose let out a gasp. "Tell me you didn't!"

Ellen couldn't contain her laughter. "Oh yes, I did. I haven't had to resort to that yet during this visit. As I said, we've reached a truce."

"Thank goodness!"

Rose's shudder had Ellen laughing again. It took her a moment before she was able to catch her breath. "I'm waiting until he does something annoying. Besides, it will have more of an effect if he's lulled into a false sense of complacency. When he no longer checks the bed before getting into it."

Jane shuddered. "I don't know how you can touch those creatures. I can scarce stand to look at them."

114

Ellen shrugged. "Castlefield coddled you too much as a child. When we used to play together, he had no problem shoving a snake in my face. I had to adapt quickly. Fortunately, you never had to deal with that."

The look of horror on Jane's face had Ellen chuckling again.

Rose shook her head, her dark curls bouncing with the motion. "You're an amazing woman, Ellen." Her expression changed, turning playful. "If His Grace wants you, make him work for it. You deserve nothing less."

Jane nodded her agreement. "But don't make him wait too long!"

CHAPTER 12

*C*ASTLEFIELD LED THE WAY to his study, where there would be little chance of being over-heard. Despite the fact his friend had just arrived, Castlefield had no doubt about the subject of their upcoming conversation.

Upon entering the room, which was filled with rich dark wood and comfortable furniture, Castlefield moved to a small table that sat off to one side of the door. Resting on top were a few glasses and a bottle of his favorite brandy. As Brantford lowered himself into an armchair, Castlefield poured a measure of liquor into two glasses. He handed one to his longtime friend and took the seat opposite.

Castlefield lifted his glass and took a healthy swallow before speaking. "I take it you're to thank for teaching Ellen how to defend herself."

Brantford's lips twitched, but only for a moment

before he sobered. "I thought it prudent. That and warning the bastard to whom she was married never to touch her again."

"How bad was it?" He didn't really want to know, but if Ellen had to live through it, he could hear about it. Whatever pain he felt whenever he thought of Ellen with that monster was nothing compared to what she must have endured.

"I don't know." Brantford downed his brandy and reached over to slam the empty glass onto the desk. "When she came to me that day—they'd only been married six months—she looked so defeated. Not at all like the Ellen we both know. But still, underneath the pain, her spine of steel was in place. I can't imagine what courage it took for her to come to me and ask how to keep her husband from touching her again."

"I wish I could kill him again, this time with my bare hands. My one regret is that he didn't suffer more before he died."

Brantford made a sound of disgust. "I failed her. Why did I not look into Laughton's background?"

"We were both young, still in school."

"That's no excuse. My instincts told me not to trust the man, but I foolishly thought our father would have made sure he was suitable before agreeing to hand over his daughter."

Castlefield shook his head. "There was nothing there. I looked. Some rumblings about his selfishness, but there are few people we know about whom we couldn't say the same thing."

"Really?" Brantford raised a brow. "I thought your interest in my sister was a recent development."

Castlefield didn't look away from his friend's steady gaze. "It isn't."

"When? Not when we were children, surely."

Castlefield laughed. "No. I was headstrong back then and definitely not interested in pursuing anyone romantically. All I cared about was horses and besting you. You're two years my junior, and I hated how effortlessly everything came to you."

Brantford lifted a shoulder in a small shrug but he allowed a smile, which told Castlefield that his friend had enjoyed their youthful rivalry as much as he had.

"I didn't really see Ellen as a woman worth pursuing until that year we came back from Oxford, after she'd already accepted Laughton's suit."

Brantford released a breath. "Your timing couldn't have been worse."

Castlefield's lips twisted in a bitter smile. "That's the tale of my life. I almost fell over when Ellen ran outside to greet you. I could scarce believe she was the same girl I'd once considered a friend and then a nuisance."

Brantford was silent a moment before saying, "I didn't realize. I remember thinking your behavior was odd, but I thought it was because you didn't know how to deal with Ellen as a woman instead of the girl you teased ruthlessly."

"You're right about my not knowing what to do about the new Ellen. She completely addled my senses."

Brantford shook his head. "And I thought I was observant. How did I miss that?"

"When I learned almost immediately upon seeing her again that Ellen was betrothed, no one could have dragged the truth from me. I didn't allow myself to think about her like that again. And then when that mess happened with Jane…" He shook his head. "Ellen needed time to deal with the death of her husband. It wasn't the time to think about pursuing her."

"But now it is."

"Just so." Castlefield tossed back the rest of his drink. The empty glass joined Brantford's on the desk.

Brantford's next words drew him from his somber thoughts. "Has she drawn one of her weapons on you?"

At least his friend had waited to bring up the subject of weapons so he wouldn't choke. "She actually carries a dagger? I thought you were just having one over on me when you mentioned that in your letter."

A corner of Brantford's mouth lifted. "She carries a dagger on her person—I'll leave it to you to discover where—and a pistol in her reticule when she needs one. Don't fret, if you haven't seen them by now, that means she won't kill you. Perhaps."

Castlefield weighed that information with great care. He wasn't surprised to learn Ellen carried weapons when she helped her brother with his missions, but would she really have a dagger on her person at all times? Even here, when they were en famille?

He couldn't help asking. "Surely she wouldn't have a weapon on her now?"

Brantford lifted a shoulder in a maddening nonresponse. It looked like he'd have to find the answer to that question himself. Hopefully, if she did carry a blade, he wouldn't discover that fact because she was holding it at his throat.

"Perhaps I should receive some of those lessons in defense as well. Normally I'd say I could handle myself in most situations, but I've seen some of those mystifying moves of yours. If you've taught Ellen even a fraction of them, I'm doomed." He wouldn't admit that the woman in question had already tossed him onto his back as easily as she would a doll.

Brantford laughed. "We'll arrange something. I wouldn't want you to be killed because you dodged the wrong way."

Castlefield knew his friend was poking fun at him. He'd never raise a hand to Ellen, and despite how much he might aggravate her on occasion, she'd never hurt him. Well, not too badly.

When his friend's laughter died, he became serious again. Too serious. Castlefield knew what was coming. He took possession of his glass again and walked over to the small table to pour himself another measure of brandy.

Brantford waited until he'd downed that second glass before speaking. "You need to tell Ellen what happened."

Castlefield had considered telling her the truth, but he couldn't tell her about the duel. She'd want to know the reason behind it, and he'd promised never to reveal that.

He itched to have another drink, but it was far too early for that. Besides, he needed his wits about him when it came to Ellen.

"I can't. I made a vow… as did you."

Brantford's eyes narrowed the tiniest fraction. Enough to tell Castlefield that he didn't appreciate the reminder. "I don't forget my promises. But my sister needs to know what really happened back then. Perhaps if you speak to Jane—"

"I'm not about to raise this subject with my sister. She's moved on and is happy again, especially now that her friendship with Ellen has been restored. I'm not going to jeopardize her happiness. It took her a long time to get over what almost happened."

"Ellen needs to know."

Deuce take it, did the man never blink? He'd never been on the receiving end of his friend's stare when he wanted something, and it was unnerving. He could see why Brantford was so good at his job. If this was even a fraction of what his enemies went through when he questioned them, they didn't stand a chance.

"When the time is right, I'll tell Ellen myself. But it's too soon. She's barely tolerating my presence."

"You're giving me excuses."

"Yes, I am. You know as well as I that courting your sister is a delicate business. As you pointed out, it's a miracle she hasn't tried to gut me yet. Let me make some progress—show her that we can be good together—before I tell her how her husband really died."

"We both know she didn't mourn his death. Whatever feelings she had for Laughton died during the first months of their marriage."

"Good. I just hope that if I can get her to accept me, any newfound feelings she might discover won't suffer a similar death when I tell her the truth."

CHAPTER 13

To SAY THE DOWAGER DUCHESS was displeased when she returned home from her visit to find Lord Brantford and his new wife had arrived while she was out paying a social call would be a vast understatement. Ellen found it amusing to watch the chagrin cross Castlefield's face when his mother chastised him over dinner for keeping their impending arrival a secret. Still, from the twinkle in his eyes when he glanced at Ellen, it was clear he had no regrets about his subterfuge.

Dinner was a lively affair. And afterward the group retired to the salon. Jane and Lord Eddings had gone upstairs to spend some time with their children before they turned in for the night, but they promised to join them later.

Brantford took it upon himself to smooth over Her Grace's annoyance with her son. It never ceased to amaze Ellen just how charming he could be when the mood struck him.

She listened as he shared an abbreviated version of the circumstances leading up to his hasty marriage to Rose before he moved on to share some amusing tales about just how far some had gone to gain his approval this past spring.

Rose, who sat next to her on the settee, leaned closer and lowered her voice so only Ellen could hear. "All that time I was trying and failing to gain Lucien's attention, I never imagined he could be so amusing. I'm torn between feeling sad all of society will never see this side of him and being relieved that is the case. I've seen the looks other women cast his way. They'd never cease their pursuit if they realized what lay beneath his icy exterior."

Ellen held back a wince. "Please don't share any details with me."

Rose smiled, and much to Ellen's dismay lowered her voice even further. "Let's just say your brother is far from unaffected in the bedchamber."

Ellen twisted her mouth in an exaggerated frown, spurring Rose to let out an unladylike snort before she raised a hand to cover her mouth. Ellen had known that Rose and her brother were well suited after seeing them together, but she still found it impossible to believe what her new sister-in-law seemed to be suggesting. She'd certainly never enjoyed any of the intimacy she and her husband had shared before she'd finally banished him from her bedroom.

Rose's gaze drifted to Castlefield before returning to Ellen. "Maybe you can find a similar happiness close by?"

Ellen shook her head. "Not you as well. You should know that not everyone seeks to wed."

If there was one thing Ellen had discovered during the brief time she'd known Rose, it was that the young woman sitting beside her was very observant.

Rose placed a hand on her arm and gave it a brief squeeze. "You weren't happy in your marriage."

"No," Ellen said, letting out a soft sigh. "But that is a subject for another time."

"I understand." Rose tilted her head and seemed to look right through her. "But I've noticed the way he keeps looking at you when your attention is elsewhere."

It took everything in her not to glance at the man in question. "You're being ridiculous. He's probably just planning how best to annoy me."

Ellen decided it was prudent to change the subject before Rose could comment further. Being the focus of speculation had never sat well with her. It was bad enough people were thinking about her and Castlefield as a potential romantic pairing, and she wasn't about to discuss it with Rose or Jane. Especially since his continued insistence on pursuing her was causing her more than a little confusion.

"How are your parents?"

Rose's smile lit her entire face. "Wonderful, thank goodness. Lucien was able to prove that my father was blackmailed into confessing to treason. The real culprit almost succeeded in escaping detection."

Ellen drew Rose into a brief hug. "My brother shared the details of your trip with me. You were very brave."

"I think the word you're looking for is *foolish*. Lucien told me to stay at the inn, but I ignored him and headed to my family's estate. Where, of course, Lord Standish was waiting for me. If Lucien hadn't arrived in time…" She gave a small shudder.

"My brother has excellent instincts. Although it wasn't his wisest decision to leave you alone at the inn. You're hardly one to sit still when you could be acting. And you had no idea Lord Standish would be waiting for you. How could you?"

"Well, I can tell you that's the last time I ever go against my husband's advice."

"I plan to hold you to that."

Their heads whipped up, and they saw Brantford now stood next to the settee. His gaze rested on his wife with censure, but it was impossible not to see the affection in his pale blue eyes.

Rose let out an exaggerated sigh, and Ellen couldn't hold back her amusement. Her brother never forgot anything, and she had no doubt Rose would come to regret that statement.

The dowager duchess stood then, followed by Castlefield.

"I've enjoyed this evening very much." Her smile included Rose, Brantford, and her. Her eyes narrowed slightly when she glanced at her son, and it was clear that he wasn't yet forgiven for his earlier transgression. "I'll see you all tomorrow."

She swept from the room amid a chorus of "good evenings."

"You survived that relatively unscathed." Brantford didn't hide his amusement.

Castlefield's gaze met hers for a moment before he replied. "I hope to make it up to her soon enough."

When he looked away, Rose nudged Ellen with her shoulder. Ellen didn't rise to her friend's teasing. She opted, instead, for another change of subject.

"We should play a hand of whist." She stood and moved to the table that had been set up in the corner of the room for that purpose.

"Shall we play men against the women?" Castlefield asked.

Ellen shook her head. "It's been a number of years since Brantford and I partnered."

Rose shook her head as she joined them. "No one would have a chance if the two of you played together. The only fair partnership is for me to claim my husband and allow the two of you"—she nodded toward Ellen and Castlefield—"to form the second pair."

Brantford regarded his wife with cool speculation. "Are you any good?"

Rose shook her head, her grin widening. "I'm horrible at cards. But since I imagine you're quite good given how these two are fighting over you, I'm sure we'll balance each other out. Give someone else a chance to best you for once."

A corner of Brantford's mouth lifted. "I'm quite formidable. I'm sure I can bring you up to scratch." He drew out a chair for his wife, his smug expression enough to be insufferable.

Castlefield groaned and drew back another chair for Ellen. He leaned close when Ellen had lowered herself into the seat. "I'm sure that together we'll be unstoppable, despite your brother's attempts to rattle us before the cards have even been dealt. I recall us being a formidable team ourselves in our younger days."

Ellen turned her head and met his gaze. "That was quite a number of years ago. I'm not sure our playing styles would suit now."

"We'll see soon enough, my lady."

CHAPTER 14

*E*LLEN WOKE WITH A SMILE on her face. With the arrival of her brother and his new wife, the last of her worries had faded away. And it turned out that Castlefield had been correct. They did make a good team.

It had been a near thing though. Despite the fact Brantford and Rose had never played whist together, they'd almost come out ahead, thanks in large part to her brother's skill. And even though the two had only been wed for such a short time, they'd already developed a knack for knowing what the other was thinking. She'd lost count of how many times a slight frown on her brother's face had kept Rose from making a disastrous move that would have cost them the game. But in the end, she and Castlefield had emerged victorious.

Rose admitted defeat after that game, pleading

tiredness after their long day. She and Brantford took their leave when Jane and Lord Eddings returned from their visit to the nursery shortly after the game had ended. They'd played another hand of whist, with Ellen and Castlefield continuing as a team against Jane and her husband, and had come out victorious a second time.

The sly glance Jane cast her way said everything when Castlefield commented again on what a good team they made.

With a stretch, Ellen reached for the bellpull by the headboard to summon a maid. Her fingers had just touched the braided rope when her gaze landed on a box wrapped in bright blue paper that sat atop the dressing table. It could only have been placed there sometime during the night.

She dropped her hand from the bellpull and stood, crossing the room to the table. It had slipped her mind that today was her birthday. Laughton had never remembered, and she'd had no reason to celebrate the day during her period of mourning. Brantford must have remembered and arranged for the surprise. It was just like him to have a maid slip into her room with the gift instead of giving it to her directly.

She lowered herself onto the seat before the dressing table and moved the brightly wrapped package closer. She wasn't surprised that he'd remembered blue was her favorite color.

She pulled open the blue paper with care and smiled when she revealed the beautiful box it covered. It was made of a rich red wood and etched with seashells along the edges of the lid.

She didn't think there'd be anything inside it since the box was beautiful enough to be a gift on its own. Still, she braced herself for disappointment as she lifted the lid back on its hinge. Blue silk lined the interior surface of the box, but what had her gasping with surprise was the object placed within the box.

A conch shell.

Her heart rate increased and her thoughts spun with the implications behind this gift. If she wasn't mistaken, it wasn't from her brother. No, this could only have come from Castlefield.

She lifted the shell from the box, and only then did she see the folded paper that had been placed under it. Her hands trembled slightly, and she took a deep breath as she put the conch back inside the box and unfolded the note.

Ellen,

I think it's time to return this to you. I know I used to tease you about it, but I, too, hold fond memories of the day we found this while playing on the beach in Brighton.

I'll admit that I recently took a page from your book

and made a wish on it. The fact that you're here now and we are on speaking terms tells me that you were correct in thinking it a good-luck charm.

I hope you're not past the time of hoping and dreaming about the future. If the girl who once used to make wishes upon a conch shell is still somewhere inside you, please accept this and keep it close.

—Charles

Ellen turned the shell over and saw the telltale scratch along one side that proved it was the same one they'd found so long ago.

She could scarce believe Castlefield had kept it all these years. She wasn't sure she believed he'd actually made a wish upon it—and who could have imagined he'd be so clever as to use this to pull on her heartstrings—but the fact that he'd kept it went a long way toward showing her he actually treasured their friendship.

She remembered how she'd sneaked into his bedroom at her family's estate all those years ago when he'd visited and she'd announced her betrothal to Laughton. But instead of a frog, she'd left this conch on his pillow. She hadn't needed to include a note. Leaving the seashell was a message that any hope she still held of remaining friends had disappeared.

Try as she might, she couldn't hold back the emotion that swelled within. She remembered well the fondness she'd held for the boy Castlefield had once been. Her disappointment when he'd stopped spending time with her. And, finally, her anger and feelings of betrayal when he'd told her that Laughton didn't care for her. She'd believed at the time that he meant she was unlovable, but given what he'd recently revealed, she now knew the real reason behind his angry words. He'd been jealous.

The fact that he'd held on to the shell all these years was proof that he cared for her, otherwise he would have disposed of it. Her husband certainly would have. But instead, Castlefield had kept it safe and now he was returning it to her.

The walls she'd carefully constructed around her heart now sported a crack, and that thought terrified her.

CHAPTER 15

*E*LLEN TRIED TO IGNORE the sense of anticipation she was powerless to push aside as she made her way downstairs.

When she entered the breakfast room, everyone was already present. Even Castlefield, who'd normally eaten and gone for what she'd learned was his daily ride by the time she was up. His gaze was intent, and she realized he was trying to discern whether she'd opened his gift. She toyed with the idea of letting him wonder a little longer, but in the end decided he deserved nothing less than honesty.

The only unoccupied seat in the room was beside Castlefield, and she couldn't help but wonder if he'd arranged for that to be the case.

"Thank you for your gift," she said after taking her seat. "It's been many years since anyone has remembered my birthday."

Brantford, who was seated opposite, raised a brow. "I thought you no longer celebrated your birthday."

A corner of Castlefield's mouth lifted. "Just doing my part to make you look bad, old man."

"Now children, don't argue." The duchess's exaggerated frown had everyone in the room laughing.

Jane looked toward one of the footmen, giving her head a slight nod. The man left the room to return a few moments later with another wrapped gift.

"I wasn't sure if we'd be doing this now or later, but since my brother already made the rest of us look bad, I can't wait." At her words, the footman handed the small package to Ellen.

"This was completely unnecessary—" Ellen began.

"No, it wasn't," Brantford said. "It's about time you started allowing others to show they care for you." He reached into a breast pocket inside his coat and removed a slim package.

Ellen couldn't conceal her surprise. "What were you saying about not celebrating my birthday?"

Brantford's tone remained even as he said, "I am, as always, prepared for any eventuality."

Rose placed a hand over her husband's, and he turned to smile at her. Emotion threatened to clog Ellen's throat at the obvious sign of affection between the newly married couple.

She opened Jane's gift first, letting out a small gasp when she saw that it contained a pair of silver hair combs, accentuated with an ornate blue-and-white enamel pattern. Her gaze met Jane's. "Is this…?" At her friend's nod, she gave her head a small shake. "But you love these."

"I love you more," Jane said. "And I'm so happy to have you back in my life."

Tears threatened at her friend's sweet words. To keep them at bay, she turned next to her brother's gift. As she looked down at the long, slim box, she realized she knew what it would contain.

She met Brantford's gaze, wondering whether this could be a mistake. At his nod of encouragement, she opened the box. Nestled within the snowy white satin that lined the interior, she found a simple gold necklace with a large teardrop-shaped sapphire. It had been her mother's favorite necklace because it was the first gift Ellen and Brantford's father had given her. Ellen had always loved that necklace, but she'd assumed it would go to her brother's wife.

She didn't bother to hide the tears that glistened in her eyes as she thanked him. He replied with one of his rare, genuine smiles.

Unable to help herself, she turned again to meet Castlefield's gaze. She wasn't sure what she'd expected to see when her eyes met his, but it wasn't the warmth and affection that radiated from him. An affection that she now realized she'd never once seen on her husband's face, not even when he'd been courting her. Laughton had won her with slick displays and honeyed words, but when she'd looked at him, she'd never seen what was so evident to her now.

Castlefield was not at all like her former husband. Unless she'd taken complete leave of her senses, it was obvious that the man seated beside her truly cared for her. They'd been friends once. Was it possible they could become more?

CHAPTER 16

*E*LLEN WAS ON EDGE all morning, her emotions threatening to overwhelm her. She could only blame her lack of control on the stark realization of everything she'd lost when she'd wed Laughton. Since then, her birthday had always been melancholy, and so she'd done everything in her power to act as though it was a day like any other.

Everything had changed when she'd opened Castlefield's gift. Breakfast had only served to underscore the fact that she was surrounded by friends and family who cared for her. After cutting herself off from her emotions for so long, it wasn't difficult to understand why they'd overwhelm her now.

It didn't help that she was surrounded by couples who were happy in their own marriages. Since her arrival, she'd grown accustomed to seeing the affection Jane and Lord Eddings displayed toward one another. And while she'd known that Brantford cared for Rose before they'd wed, it still brought her up short to witness it. He, the man whom everyone accused of having ice water instead of blood in his veins, was clearly in love with his wife.

Despite their former friendship and his claims to care for her, she knew she couldn't have that with Castlefield. He'd told her that he planned to court her, and he was going about it in an entirely different manner than the men who'd courted her in the past. Especially Laughton. Instead of grandiose gestures designed to showcase himself in a positive light, Castlefield seemed to care about her feelings. She imagined the fact they'd once known each other well helped him in knowing just how to approach her. If he'd pressed her harder, she would have had no difficulty spurning him.

But instead he'd challenged her, knowing she would never run from a contest of wills. And then once she arrived, he behaved like the friend she'd once known. The one she'd missed.

For the first time in twelve years, she wanted to make a birthday wish. Not for love, of course. No, she wasn't so far gone as to believe she'd ever have what the other couples had found, but perhaps she could discover just a glimmer of it. Surely the man who knew her well enough to know just how much a seashell would affect her would be able to show her that.

Still, she hesitated about approaching him. She was on her way up to the nursery, having decided that spending time with Henry and Hope would be a welcome distraction, when fate took the decision from her hands.

"Ellen?"

She looked up to find Castlefield at the top of the stairs and her breath caught in her throat. When she'd looked at him before today, she'd seen the man who used to be her childhood friend but with whom she'd developed a rivalry. The man who wanted to be friends again at the very least. But now she saw the man who could show her what it was to be loved. Even if she didn't believe they could have a future together, she realized that she trusted him enough to ask him to show her what Jane and Rose had found. Happiness in a man's arms.

"Is something the matter?" he asked when she reached the top of the stairs. His brows were drawn together. "Your brother told me you don't like celebrating your birthday. Did I misstep in giving you that gift?"

When she met his dark brown eyes and saw the concern reflected there, a pang of longing almost took away her breath. And if she wasn't mistaken, she detected a similar yearning in his eyes.

"I don't want hearts and flowers," she said.

He stilled and waited for her to continue.

Taking a deep breath, she opened herself up. "I

want you to show me everything I've been missing. Everything I never had with Laughton."

She didn't have to elaborate further. Castlefield knew exactly what she meant. She wanted him to show her the physical pleasure a man and woman could have together.

A corner of his mouth turned up and the guarded expression left his eyes.

Ellen's traitorous heart threatened to kick, but she ignored it. She could be practical even if she'd allowed her emotions to lead her in coming to this decision.

With all the rumors she'd started about him and his wild ways, she would have heard if Castlefield shared Laughton's penchant for hurting women. On the chance her instincts were wrong about that fact, logic said her brother would never have remained good friends with him if that was the case. Brantford had grown in ruthlessness over the years, and she doubted there was a secret any man possessed that he didn't know or couldn't discover.

As she looked into Castlefield's eyes, she knew with absolute certainty that he'd never hurt her. Not physically, at any rate. No, the danger would be to her emotions if she wasn't careful. Castlefield was going to show her that physical pleasure could exist between a man and a woman, nothing more. There would be no marriage, no children. No happily-ever-after for her. And most important, any dalliance the two of them shared would be over long before he tired of her.

She ignored the traitorous corner of her heart that yearned for more. That desire would never be fulfilled. Unlike Rose and Jane, who were both so open and loving with their husbands, Ellen was incapable of sharing herself so freely. Laughton had killed that side of her. But that didn't mean she wouldn't reach out and grasp the opportunity to experience even a faint shadow of that happiness. Just for this one small moment in time.

He took several steps down the hallway and Ellen followed.

"I didn't mean now," she said, aiming for a levity she was far from feeling.

He stopped and looked down at her, his eyes dancing with amusement. "I'm not presuming as much. But since I found myself flat on my back the last time I attempted to kiss you, I thought it prudent to move away from the stairs."

She knew he was trying to make her laugh, but she was still embarrassed by her overreaction. He'd been correct in what he'd told her then. If this was ever going to happen, she needed to be the one to initiate it.

He remained still as she closed the small distance between them. "It's been a long time since I've kissed a man."

His eyes darkened and the levity had disappeared.

The tension that surrounded them now was not one born from animosity but from anticipation. Her nerves were stretched taut, and the heat in his eyes told her that he felt the same way.

Finally he broke the silence. "There can never be any doubt between us that you want this as much as I do."

Ellen was powerless to look away as she placed her hands on his shoulders. "No."

She rose onto her toes. Only then did he lower his head, but still he held back.

Emotion she dared not examine too closely had her closing the last inch that separated them and pressing her mouth against his. When he didn't move to deepen the kiss after several seconds, she started to step back but found the movement hampered by his hands on her waist. Their eyes met.

"Do you trust me, Ellen?"

She nodded.

He took her mouth then in a kiss that was unlike any she'd ever had. But almost as soon as it started, heat beginning to dance along her skin, he released her.

Her breath was unsteady, and they stood like that for what seemed an eternity, their eyes locked in a silent battle of wills that spoke of their mutual desire to continue.

He took a step back but didn't look away. "I'm in the master bedroom now."

This time it was her turn to smile in wicked amusement. "I know. I make it a habit to learn the terrain of my enemies. Just in case I should need to leave a little present for you on your pillow."

The sound of Castlefield's laughter lingered in the air as he turned and continued downstairs.

CHAPTER 17

Try as he might to temper his expectations, Castlefield couldn't hold back the anticipation that surged through his veins as he thought about the night ahead. Tension coiled within him as he paced the length of his bedroom, clad only in trousers and a shirt. He'd removed his cravat and waistcoat and now waited with barely concealed impatience for Ellen's arrival.

Twelve long years had passed since he realized he no longer saw her as a childhood friend but as a woman about whom he cared a great deal. But that discovery had come too late for him to act on it.

He'd tried to warn her away from Laughton when he realized they were betrothed, but instead of keeping his calm, he'd hurled hateful insults about the man. The revelation of his feelings had left him off-balance, and it hadn't occurred to him Ellen would be hurt by his words.

He wasn't proud of his behavior, but he'd been young—just twenty—and unequipped to deal with the stark realization that he couldn't have everything he wanted. He was heir to a dukedom, and everywhere he went, women cast themselves at him. He'd availed himself of those who were older and more experienced than he, being careful to stay clear of those who wanted marriage. He'd always expected that when he did marry, it would be to someone he liked and respected. He'd never counted on love. The fact that he'd felt the stirrings of that emotion whenever he looked at Ellen that summer long ago had him wanting to howl with rage at the unfairness of the situation.

He accepted that he bore more than a modicum of blame for the estrangement that had grown between them since then. He hadn't been able to even look at Ellen after she'd wed Laughton. At first it was a relief when she no longer visited his family's estate in Sussex for the summer, but after what nearly happened to Jane, he couldn't bear to think about what Ellen might have suffered at that monster's hands.

He'd allowed her to spread rumors about him without bothering to correct them. In a perverse way he couldn't even begin to understand, he took a measure of satisfaction in knowing she still thought about him. Although he hadn't exaggerated when he told Ellen that the lies she'd spread about his lasciviousness had only served to make him popular in certain circles. Circles where the women would never expect or demand a proposal of marriage from a duke.

But now it was time for all that to change. He was no longer the impulsive youth he'd once been. He would have to be patient with Ellen to gain her trust. That she'd even entertained the notion of the two of them being together was more than he'd expected, although he hoped for much more than that. He wanted everything with her. She wasn't ready for that yet, but if he was patient he might just gain all the things he'd once believed lost to him forever.

He was so immersed in his own thoughts that he almost didn't hear the soft knock at the bedroom door. Rolling his shoulders and schooling his features so he wouldn't scowl if he found a hapless servant on the other side of the door, he crossed the room and opened it.

It wasn't something a man would readily admit, but his heart threatened to soar right out of his chest when he found Ellen standing in the hallway. She'd changed into her nightdress, but her modesty was preserved by a lavender dressing gown that covered her from the base of her neck to the floor. He didn't speak, but he imagined his smile spoke volumes as he stepped back and allowed her to enter.

She didn't hesitate, sailing past him and turning to watch as he closed the door behind her.

He hesitated, torn between not wanting to give Ellen cause to change her mind but also wanting to ensure they wouldn't be interrupted. He wouldn't put it past Brantford to come strolling into his bedroom just to cause mischief if he knew Ellen was here. But then again, it wasn't as though a lock would keep him out if that was his intention.

"You can lock it. I'm more than capable of unlocking a door and showing myself out if I wish to leave."

He could sense her amusement as he turned to do that. When he faced her again, words failed him as he took her in. The blond mass of her hair was unbound, falling well past her shoulders. He had to fight back the urge to thread his fingers through it and lose himself in the kiss he longed to share with her.

She tilted her head, waiting for him to speak, and he had to clear his throat before he could do so. "I wasn't sure you'd come."

"I'm a woman of my word. If I tell you I'll be somewhere, then nothing short of an emergency would stop me."

The hint of steel in her voice told him he'd blundered, but not too badly. She'd have no qualms about brushing past him and walking out if he'd truly angered her.

"Forgive me," he said, taking great care to clasp

his hands behind his back so he wouldn't reach for her and botch things further by rushing. "It wasn't so much that I doubted your word but my own worthiness. I know I'm not your favorite person. It seemed almost too much to hope that I could actually have you."

"You don't have me."

"Not yet, no. I'm well aware of that fact. But at least I now have hope that will change one day."

She narrowed her eyes and stared at him for several intense seconds. Castlefield remained silent throughout her perusal. He'd take his cue as to how to behave from what she said next.

"You didn't seem to have any misgivings when you first approached me, nor on any other occasion since."

"Oh, I had more than a few doubts," he said. "But I try not to let them direct my actions. Fortune favors the bold, after all."

"Indeed," she said. "Along that vein…"

He watched as she reached for the sash of her dressing gown and untied it. He thought she'd stop there, but when she shrugged out of the garment and allowed it to fall to the floor in a soft puddle of fabric, he thought he'd lose his mind. The nightgown was white and modest in cut, but the light from several candles lit her from behind and he could clearly see the shape of her figure through the thin material. The curve of her hips, normally hidden behind the straight fall of the skirts of current fashion, was clearly outlined for his view, and he wanted nothing more than to take hold of them and draw her closer.

When he dragged his gaze back up to her face, stopping along the way to take in the shape of her breasts, the defiant tilt of her jaw told him exactly what Ellen was doing. It also served as a reminder to rein in his desires. She was trying to be brave and take control of the situation, which meant she was afraid. He needed to get his emotions in check before he found himself on his back again with her fleeing the room.

He glanced at the bed but discarded that location. When he'd originally planned this seduction, he hadn't realized how close to the edge he'd be. If Ellen joined him in his bed, he wasn't sure he'd be strong enough to keep from claiming her. But their first time together couldn't be about him. He had to show her he could be an unselfish lover, capable, first and foremost, of bringing her pleasure.

Something deep within roared in displeasure at that thought, but he ignored it. Ellen would only be his on her own terms.

He held out his hand and waited. After several seconds, she placed her hand in his. The air had cooled with the setting of the sun, and given how little she was wearing, he wasn't surprised to find her skin was cold. He didn't comment on it, however. He'd soon warm her up.

He turned toward his dressing room.

She hesitated, glancing at the bed and then back at him. "Where are we going?"

"We need a change of scenery."

He caught a glimpse of relief on her face and silently pledged he would wipe away all her unpleasant memories of hurried, one-sided couplings in her marital bed. But today would not be that day.

"Grab one of those candlesticks, please" he said, nodding toward the one that had served to offer him a tantalizing view of her figure. It held three lit candles. Not nearly enough in his mind, but at least they wouldn't be fumbling around in the dark.

He didn't release her hand as he opened the door to his dressing room, where a chaise longue took up a prominent place in the center of the dark space. He couldn't recall a time he'd ever used it, but now he was glad for its presence. He took the candelabra from Ellen and placed it on a tall set of drawers that rested against one wall. The candles cast a warm glow over the room, at the same time lengthening the shadows. He and Ellen would do this again one day, and he'd make sure to light the room with as many candles and lamps as he could find. But for today he hoped the shadows would allow Ellen a measure of security.

She tugged her hand from his, and with regret he allowed it. To his shock, she bent slightly at the waist and began to drag up her nightgown with her right hand. He was transfixed as he watched each inch of skin appear. When the material passed her right knee, he clenched his hands to keep from reaching out for her. He'd have to stop her soon, however. This wasn't at all what he'd planned.

A black garter came into view on her right thigh, and he began imagining the skin that lay above it and how smooth it would feel to the touch. He held himself tightly in check as he watched her turn to the left. It was only then that he noticed the sheath strapped to the garter on the outside of her thigh.

His mouth dropped open when she unclasped the sinister strip of fabric and allowed her nightdress to fall back into place. He caught the unmistakable hilt of a dagger sticking out from the garter that had been strapped to her leg seconds before and found himself staring at the weapon for several seconds.

"I'd convinced myself Brantford was in jest about that," he said when he was finally capable of speech again.

Ellen grinned as she pulled the dagger from its sheath and twirled it with swift, deft movements between her fingers. "My brother never jests about safety."

She threw the knife, and it landed solidly within the doorframe, embedded several inches deep.

"I didn't think it was possible to be any more aroused than I already was."

The words were out before he realized he was

saying them aloud. Ellen's gaze dipped to his trousers and her expression shuttered.

He watched as she straightened her back and turned toward the chaise. If she imagined he was going to have her lie down while he rutted away on top of her, she was sadly mistaken. He reached for her hand again and brought her around to face him.

"I'm not foolish enough to believe you require that dagger to stop me."

She smiled, no doubt remembering how she'd so easily flipped him onto his back the first time he'd tried to kiss her. "I'm not going to stop you."

He searched her face for any sign of doubt. "Be absolutely sure about this, Ellen."

Her gaze lowered to his mouth, and he had to hold back a groan as she whispered, "I am."

CHAPTER 18

*H*E LOWERED HIS HEAD and she rose up onto her toes. They met somewhere in the middle, and he didn't hold back his murmur of pleasure. This wasn't their first kiss, but it was the most satisfying. As he'd longed to do when she first entered his bedroom, he buried his hands in her hair and tilted her head to the side so he could gain better access to her mouth.

She stiffened when he touched his tongue to her lips but opened for him after a moment. He moved slowly, drawing out the pleasure for both her and himself. The way she melted against him when he stroked his tongue along hers told him that she did find pleasure in his kiss. The soft mewl she made at the back of her throat was almost his undoing.

"Ellen..." His voice was rough as he tore his

mouth away and began to rain soft kisses along her throat. "I want to show you so much."

She took a deep breath before replying. "That's why I'm here."

But the slight tremor in her voice had betrayed her—she was still nervous about what was to come. Unfortunately, he was powerless to reassure her with words alone. He'd have to show her that he could be trusted. When they finally did come together, she would be as eager to consummate their union as he.

He straightened and looked down at her. "Forget all your expectations. I'm going to touch you now, but I promise I won't hurt you or rush through this to reach my own satisfaction. If I do anything you don't like or that causes you any distress, you have only to tell me and I'll stop."

He waited for her nod of assent before bringing his mouth to hers again. She liked kissing him, so he'd start there.

His emotions soared when she responded with eagerness. Holding her against him, feeling the way she came alive in his arms, tested his self-control to the breaking point. But he'd vowed to make tonight all about her, and he meant to see that through.

He shifted, bringing her along with him, until the backs of his calves hit the chaise longue. Hoping the sudden change in their positions wouldn't frighten the delightful woman in his arms into fleeing, he lowered himself onto it. At the same time, he shifted Ellen slightly to the side so she was sitting across his lap. He was careful not to settle her onto his aching erection, however.

Ellen's breath caught in her throat when she registered the change in their positions, but her mouth never left his. It took only a moment before she settled more fully against him, and his heart stuttered when she took control of their kiss. He allowed it, knowing instinctively that this was the first time she'd ever done so. The way she ran her hands across the breadth of his shoulders caused him to lose focus. He'd long imagined Ellen touching him. That she was doing so now over his shirt didn't matter. Ellen was on his lap, kissing him with enthusiasm, and that was enough. One day soon, he vowed silently, they'd be skin-to-skin.

Continuing to move slowly so he wouldn't alarm her, he placed one hand on her knee, expecting her to stiffen. Instead, she made another soft sound of assent before pulling back.

She glanced down at his hand and then back at him. "You're not going to get far touching me over my nightdress."

"You'd be surprised what can happen over one's clothing."

She gave her head a small shake, but her lips curled at his gentle teasing. "I don't believe you."

He grinned back at her. "That is a challenge I'll readily accept another day. As for now…"

He kissed her again, and her response told him she found pleasure in his touch as he moved his hand below the fabric of her nightgown, slowly inching his fingers along the inside of her thigh. Lust coursed through him when he discovered she wasn't wearing any undergarments. The heat of her skin urged him to continue.

When he reached the top of her thigh, she didn't open for him, but she didn't stop him either. She might not be an innocent, but she clearly had no knowledge of everything a man and woman could do together.

He pulled her leg to one side. She allowed the movement but let out a soft gasp of surprise when he touched her between them.

"Have you ever touched yourself here?" he asked as he moved his fingers along the length of her slit. He felt her heat first, then moisture. She was enjoying this as much as he'd known she would.

She caught her bottom lip between her teeth before nodding. He almost said something flippant but held back the urge. This was Ellen as he'd never seen her—vulnerable and open to him. There would be plenty of time for her to discover there could be light teasing in the bedroom, but right now he wanted her to concentrate on the enjoyment she was experiencing.

Her hands were anchored around his neck, holding her stable as he caressed her breast with his other hand. She began to shift away from his touch but stopped when he brushed a finger over the pearl that rested at the top of her folds. When she arched into him, he took her mouth again, intent on completing his assault on her senses.

This time it was she who tore her mouth away, but he could tell from the flush on her face and her ragged breathing that she was close. He redoubled his movements and her breath caught. He could only stare at her in awe when she closed her eyes and let out a small keening cry as she reached her peak. He didn't even care that she was squeezing his neck so tightly she threatened to leave bruises.

He stopped his onslaught on her senses, then and cradled her fully against him, one hand stroking along the length of her back. His own breathing was not as steady as he would have liked.

He waited as her heartbeat slowed to a more normal rhythm and her breaths steadied, using the time to rein in his frustration. He was still hard and knew she'd be able to feel it where she remained curled around him on his lap. Her arms loosened from their tight grip and soft gasps of air tickled the side of his throat.

"Was that all?"

He didn't have to see her face to know she was confused. "That wasn't enough? We can always do it again."

She let out a soft sigh and lifted her head to meet

his gaze. "It's been my experience that men care more about their own pleasure that that of the woman with whom they lie."

He wanted to scowl at the reminder of all she must have suffered at the hands of her husband, but he forced himself to keep his expression neutral when he replied. "I've already told you that you haven't been with the right man."

"Is that what you are? The right man?"

He smiled in response. When she made a slight scoffing sound, he couldn't stop from barking out a laugh. "I am definitely the right man for you."

She considered his reply for several seconds. "So we won't be doing anything more tonight?"

She was so adorable when she was confused, and he couldn't resist the urge to rub his nose against hers. "No, Ellen, we won't. But I promise you there are more delights in store for you."

"What makes you think I'll be back for more? I've already had my satisfaction. My curiosity has been sated."

He groaned at her not-so-subtle reminder that she was the only one who'd reached completion. He'd have to take himself in hand later, or there would be no chance of his falling asleep.

He stroked one hand along the inside of her thigh again, stopping before reaching the top. Ellen's soft moan in response told him everything he needed to know.

He lowered his head to meet her gaze, desire surging to a conflagration when she closed her eyes and waited for his mouth to claim hers. Somehow he held himself back from doing just that. "That was but the beginning, my love. You have no idea what I have planned for you. And we both know your curiosity knows no bounds. You'll be back."

Her eyes opened, and she met his gaze for several moments before resting her head against his shoulder. That small movement told him, without the need for words, that she trusted him.

They remained like that for a full minute before she finally took a shuddering breath and rose from his lap. His arms tightened in reflex around her, but in the end he allowed her to stand. The fabric of her nightdress fell to cover her legs. He would never be able to constrain this woman—not that he had any desire to. She had to come to him entirely of her own volition or not at all.

She looked down at where he remained seated on the chaise longue. "What are you doing to me, Charles?"

"I'm wooing you, Ellen."

He could see that she finally believed him. This wasn't a game to him. But instead of pleasure, he saw a hint of fear cross her features. He wanted to soothe away that fear. Instead, he said nothing when she pulled away from him and, without a word, left the dressing room. He remained frozen on the chaise, listening as she paused briefly. He imagined she was donning her robe in that moment.

Then, far too soon, she unlocked and opened his bedroom door, and he heard the soft click of it closing behind her.

CHAPTER 19

*E*LLEN MADE IT BACK to her room without encountering anyone. It wasn't her first clandestine trip to Castlefield's bedroom, but the goal of those visits had been to vex him. This time she'd had a very different purpose for visiting his bedroom and a much different result. She couldn't deny that the encounter had left her more than a little shaken.

She'd prepared her normal pretext if anyone saw her—she was sneaking down to the kitchens to have more of whatever it was they'd had for dessert that evening. But now her thoughts were scattered, and she couldn't even remember what that had been.

The thought of trying to stumble through her prepared excuse while thoughts of what she'd just done with Charles ran through her mind threatened to bring heat to her face. She hadn't blushed since she was a maiden, and perhaps not even then.

Fortunately, all the guests were housed in the same wing as the family and she didn't have to travel far before reaching the safety of her bedroom. She let herself in and turned the key in the lock.

It was impossible not to think about their encounter as she removed her dressing gown and settled between the sheets of the four-poster bed. When she closed her eyes, the memories intensified, and she could almost feel his touch on her skin. More than that, she yearned for it.

When she'd left his room, she'd almost expected him to try to prevent her. And if the truth were known, she wouldn't have been able to stop him if he'd tried to press for more. Not because he was stronger than her and could force himself upon her. No, if he'd pressed for more, she would have given it to him willingly.

His parting words had left her more unsettled than anything he'd done. Those words had come as a pleasant surprise because now she knew he wasn't playing a game. Why else would he take such care to give her a glimpse of the delights that could be had between a man and a woman without taking any of those delights for himself?

He was in earnest when he told her he was wooing her, and that terrified her.

Even as the thought entered her mind, she knew it wasn't correct. She wasn't frightened of him or his intentions. She was hopeful. Possibly even teetering on the edge of falling into an ill-conceived infatuation with him.

The last time that had happened, she'd been young and naive and had truly believed Laughton loved her. What he'd loved, however, was her body, though he'd never taken such care with it. He'd also loved being aligned with the Brantfords through marriage, although that connection hadn't served him well in the end. No, after her brother had learned the extent of her misery, he'd taken her under his wing—issuing a solo invitation for her to visit him that Laughton had been unable to deny—and shown her how to incapacitate her husband should he try to hurt her again. The lessons on how to handle a dagger had come later, after Brantford had inherited.

Brantford's warnings that he would have no qualms about ruining Laughton if he ever touched her again had done the rest. Her husband had abandoned the physical side of their marriage and soothed his male pride by seducing other women. She'd welcomed their separation and told herself she was content never to bear children if it meant she no longer had to endure her husband's attentions.

But now Charles was stirring up all those dreams she'd carefully tucked away. It didn't help that she was surrounded by couples who were in love. If her brother, of all people, could find happiness in marriage, why couldn't she? And she wasn't that old. Women her age and older had children with alarming regularity, though she'd been told it was much more difficult once one was past the first bloom of youth.

Huffing out an exasperated sigh, Ellen rolled over and hugged a second pillow. As she drifted off to sleep, she tried not to be too hard on herself when she began to imagine she was hugging Charles. When the sun rose the following morning, she'd go back to her normal, practical self.

CHAPTER 20

*U*NFORTUNATELY, KEEPING her wayward emotions in check proved to be harder than she expected. As the days passed, it became increasingly difficult to hide the fact she and Charles had grown closer. Jane, for one, had noticed a change in their relationship. Ellen was certain, however, that her friend didn't suspect she was spending a portion of her nights with him. If she did, Jane never would have been able to contain her joy and would have questioned Ellen about their future long before now.

The same couldn't be said for her own brother. Ellen had noticed several significant glances between Brantford and Charles. And given her brother's uncanny ability to uncover secrets, she wouldn't be surprised if he knew exactly what was happening. She certainly wasn't going to raise the subject with him, however. As long as no one asked her about a future wedding, she could ignore their speculation. If there was one thing Ellen was good at, after all, it was compartmentalizing her emotions.

It wasn't easy, but she was determined not to succumb to the feelings that threatened to erupt whenever she was with Charles. She'd been visiting him every night for the past week, each secret rendezvous more heated than the last, but they'd yet to make love. He'd been scrupulous each night about seeing to her pleasure and denying his own. It was clear to her he wanted to take that final step, and if she was being honest with herself, so did she. But so far he'd kept from losing control.

They were playing a dangerous game, especially when the rest of their families were present. She'd almost slipped and called him by his given name when she came down for dinner that evening, and she continually caught herself glancing his way over the meal.

As the dishes for the soup course were cleared away, she was debating whether it would be safe to smile at him without rousing the others' suspicions when she felt Jane tap her on the arm.

She turned her attention to her friend, giving her the smile she'd been thinking of bestowing on Charles.

Jane lowered her voice and glanced at Castlefield before turning to look at her again. "You're woolgathering, Ellen. Is there something you wish to share with me?"

Ellen shook her head, hating that she had to keep this secret. But the last thing she wanted was to disappoint Jane again since her relationship with Jane's brother was going to be of short duration. There was no point in saying anything that would have Jane spinning dreams of the two of them becoming sisters.

"I was thinking about Brighton," Ellen said.

That was all it took to distract Jane. In her excitement about the upcoming trip to her new home, she was all but bouncing in her seat.

"I know we're only an hour away from the sea by carriage, but I'm so happy to be moving closer to the water. We make it a point to visit the shore daily while we're there, but this will be the first year we aren't renting a house for the summer. Henry loves it as well, and he made many friends last year. Hope is still young, but I know she'll come to feel the same. I can't wait for you to follow us down."

Ellen was of two minds about her reply. She really did want to spend more time with Jane, but in that moment, she knew she'd miss her nightly visits with Charles. She smiled, saying, "I'm looking forward to it as well."

Jane sighed. "The next week will seem quiet without the whole family there. It's been so nice having a full house again. I've missed it."

Ellen reached out and squeezed Jane's hand

before releasing it again. "So have I. But I'm sure your husband will enjoy having you to himself for a little while."

Jane glanced across the table before lowering her voice and leaning closer to Ellen. "Charles doesn't normally stay longer than a day or two when he visits. He maintains that this house is near enough that he can visit the seaside whenever he so desires. Do I have you to thank for his willingness to pay us an extended visit this year?"

Jane's eyes were sparkling, and Ellen had to break eye contact, hating that she couldn't be honest with her closest friend. "His Grace is his own man. Far be it from me to try to discern the reasons behind his actions."

She couldn't resist a quick glance at the man in question. As though he could sense her gaze, he looked away from the conversation he was having with Brantford and met her eyes. She didn't realize she was smiling at him until Jane bumped their shoulders. She was thankful in that moment that she'd never been prone to blushing.

Brantford turned the conversation then, asking if much had changed in Brighton since he'd last visited several years before. That was all it took for Jane to start talking about everything she hoped to do when they joined her in a week's time.

Ellen met her brother's eyes and tipped her head

in silent thanks. The look in his eyes was all the confirmation Ellen needed. Her brother knew exactly what was happening between her and Charles.

CHAPTER 21

*E*LLEN WAS PREPARING to make her nightly trip to Castlefield's bedroom when a single knock sounded at the door. She tightened the sash of her dressing gown as she crossed the room to open the door.

She expected to find a maid. Instead, Charles stood in the hallway. One corner of his mouth tilted up in a smile that set her heart racing. Without a word, she opened the door wider to allow him to enter.

"Is there a reason for the personal escort tonight, Your Grace?" she asked, pitching her voice low. "What if someone sees us making our way to your bedroom? I don't think they'd believe we were both headed downstairs for a second helping of the syllabub."

The heat that entered his eyes caused a shiver to

race down her spine. She was in a bad way if a mere look from this man could turn her into a puddle of longing.

"I thought it might make a nice change of pace to continue our... endeavors... here tonight."

She made her agreement clear by way of locking the door before turning to face him again. "Are you sure you can keep your voice down? Unlike your chambers, my room isn't flanked by several unoccupied bedrooms, and I've made up my mind that tonight is the night you'll lose control. It's only fair, after all."

He was about to protest, but she cut him off. She'd rehearsed this speech in her head and she wouldn't be denied. "I know this was supposed to be about me. You've proven your point that not all men are selfish boors in the bedroom. But now, more than anything, I want to know what it is to make love to a man. One who doesn't just go about his business atop me and then leave the room without a word. Unless, of course, you don't think you're up to the challenge."

He caught hold of one of her hands and drew her against him. "I think you'll find that I'm more than up to the challenge." The hard press of his erection against her belly gave proof to his words. "The more important question is whether you can keep from crying out."

Ellen twined her hands through the hair at the

base of his neck. "I'm not certain I can make that promise, but I'm willing to try."

That was all the encouragement Charles needed before lowering his head and capturing her mouth in a kiss that told her without words that he was more than ready to consummate their affair.

Their lovemaking that night was surprising for reasons other than the new location. Ellen couldn't help thinking that Charles wanted to tell her something. He gazed down at her with a possessive intensity as he slid into her, and she barely remembered to clamp her teeth into her bottom lip to keep from crying out.

She'd expected roughness from him given the way he'd been abstaining from seeking his own release over the past week, but he surprised her by moving slowly. He delayed her release until she wanted to weep from frustration. She would have complained, but it was clear he was torturing himself as much as her. When she finally reached her peak, he held himself in check long enough to allow her tremors to cease before pulling out of her and finding his own end on the sheets.

He remained over her, his arms caging her head and holding his weight from crushing her. Their foreheads touched as they both struggled to catch their breath. Charles's eyes searched hers, and Ellen couldn't stop feeling she should be concerned. The way he looked at her, the care he'd taken... She couldn't help but wonder if this was to be their last night together. It was probably for the best they end things now before their friendship was compromised irrevocably—if it wasn't already—but she couldn't deny she wasn't ready to let him go. Not yet.

Charles rolled onto his side and drew Ellen against him so that her head rested on his shoulder. It was unwise of her to become so sentimental, but she closed her eyes and allowed herself to revel in the way his body felt against hers. Not even in the beginning, when her husband had first taken her after they'd wed, had she felt this close to another person. That thought should have alarmed her, but she'd deal with the repercussions later. For now she was content to enjoy the moment, knowing it would end soon. She doubted she'd ever find this sense of peace again with another.

His hands stroked over her back, their heat seeping through to her bones. She was on the edge of falling asleep when his voice broke into the silence.

"We might not be able to do this once we reach Brighton. I don't know where we'll be sleeping, and I'm not sure it would be wise to risk being caught."

Ellen lifted her head and met his gaze. "Then perhaps we shouldn't go to Brighton."

Her desire to stay right here with this man surprised her, but she didn't regret her words. In that moment she wanted nothing more than to wrest whatever happiness she could from their short time together.

"And disappoint Jane? I know you wouldn't want to do that."

Ellen sighed. Aiming for levity, she said, "Take note of this moment. I'm about to admit something you likely won't hear from my lips again, but you're correct."

His laughter rumbled through her where their bodies still touched. "Just in case we're placed at opposite ends of the house, it might be wise to make up for lost time before we join them."

In reply, Ellen traced a hand down his torso and took hold of his erection, surprised he was already hard again. If this week was to be the last time they'd have together, she planned to make the most of it.

CHAPTER 22

*C*ASTLEFIELD MADE HIS WAY back to his own bed a little before dawn. When he entered his bedroom, he didn't even glance at the bed. He wouldn't be getting any more sleep now that he'd left Ellen's side.

He'd been able to push away his guilt while he was with her, but he could no longer avoid the consequences of his actions. He'd been selfish. He'd almost convinced himself he wouldn't make love to Ellen until after he'd revealed the truth about his part in her husband's death. But when faced with the fear that she might never forgive him for keeping the secret, he'd pushed aside the inner voice that cautioned him to stop and finally claimed Ellen for his own.

Every smile she'd given him, every contented sigh, had called forth a dark certainty that this might be the last time she allowed him near her.

He'd put it off as long as he could. It was time to tell her the truth.

He couldn't tell her everything, of course. The events leading up to his duel with Laughton weren't his secret to reveal. Still, he needed to tell her that her husband hadn't died in a hunting accident but by his hand.

He should have told her everything long before now. Pure selfishness had kept him from doing so prior to their relationship becoming physical. But he knew without a doubt that telling her about their duel would have doomed any chance to show Ellen he wasn't like Laughton. That they could have something special that was vastly different from her first marriage.

He'd gambled with respect to when to tell her the truth. Now it was time to reveal what he could and hope any feelings she'd developed for him were enough to keep him from losing the woman he loved.

He was on edge, pacing in an attempt to relieve some of his disquiet when his valet entered the room at his customary time. He gave himself up to the familiarity of his morning routine and sometime later was making his way toward the breakfast room. He waited in the hallway, listening to the sounds of Jane and her family taking their leave of the other guests.

When his sister's family stepped into the hallway, he smiled in greeting and followed the group to the front hallway. Henry held Eddings's hand while Hope was perched on his sister's hip. As he said his good-byes, he tried not to think about having to say goodbye to Ellen as well.

He waited, his mother by his side, as the group stepped into the carriage that awaited outside, their excitement to finally be off to Brighton and their new estate palpable. Once the carriage started down the driveway, he returned to the breakfast room. His mother had murmured something about having letters to write before making her way upstairs.

His eyes met Ellen's as he entered the room, and he didn't miss the way they lit for a brief moment, betraying her interest, before she looked away. Rose was seated next to her with Brantford at his wife's other side.

Rose had glanced at Ellen when he entered the room, and he was sure she'd seen Ellen's reaction at his arrival. When he turned his gaze to Brantford, inclining his head in greeting, the other man gave him a solemn nod. How Brantford always knew exactly what was on his mind was a mystery he'd long since given up trying to solve.

Brantford murmured something about needing to steal his wife away for a moment, and before Castle-field fully realized the man's intent, he was alone with Ellen.

He wasn't ready for this conversation, but it was time to stop avoiding it. He dismissed the footman stationed by the sideboard with nothing more than a nod before turning to look at Ellen again.

Her brows drew together as she looked after the departing figures of her brother and his wife before she released her breath in a soft sigh.

"Brantford knows about us." She met his eyes. "Did you tell him?"

Castlefield shook his head. "There's very little that man doesn't know. But yes, he knows about my interest. I certainly didn't tell him things had progressed beyond that, though he knows I planned to court you."

"Good heavens, did you ask his permission?"

"I didn't need to. Your brother has known for some time that I care for you, though he only recently realized it went beyond friendship."

"Do you think he knows…?"

She didn't have to finish the question. "About the recent development in our relationship? I certainly didn't tell him, but in all likelihood, yes."

"I'd guessed as much, but I'd hoped I was wrong." Ellen gave her head a small shake before smiling at him. "Normally you've already broken your fast by this time and disappeared for the morning. I didn't wear you out last night, did I?"

He laughed, her expression of exaggerated innocence lifting his spirits. "It was a near thing. But no, I wanted to spend the morning with you."

He knew he was acting the coward, but he went to

the sideboard and filled a plate before returning to take the seat Rose had vacated. He moved the empty dish to the side and replaced it with his own. The food tasted like straw, but he wasn't about to give up this moment to spend time alone with Ellen.

The conversation turned to the subject of his sister's recent departure and their plans to join her in Brighton. For fifteen minutes he pretended this might not be the last civil conversation he'd ever have with this woman.

"Something is bothering you," Ellen said when he finally pushed his plate away.

"What makes you say that?"

"We've known each other many years. I don't need my brother's uncanny gift for reading people to know when you're thinking about something else. Or rather, trying hard not to think about it."

There was no point in denying it. He rose and held out a hand to her. "Let's go for a walk."

Ellen didn't even hesitate as she placed her hand in his and allowed him to help her up. He tucked her hand into his elbow and led her toward the back of the house and out to the gardens.

The rose garden had always been Ellen's favorite, and so he turned her in that direction when they emerged from the house.

Ellen didn't prod further, waiting for him to break the silence. Far too soon for his liking, they were settling onto a bench on the far side of the fragrant garden. They'd be visible to anyone looking out the windows from the house, but their conversation would be private.

"I have struggled with how to tell you this, but it can no longer wait."

Ellen looked away. She held her hands in her lap, but he didn't miss the way she clenched them together before forcing herself to relax. "I understand. We both knew our… liaison would never last. I went into this affair knowing as much."

A pang of regret pierced him. Ellen still didn't trust him. How could she not realize her own worth? Or how completely she'd captivated him?

"I don't want this to end, Ellen."

Her head swung toward him, her eyes wide. "Please don't propose. I'm not ready for that. I don't know if I will ever be."

He wished that convincing her to marry him was the only thing on his mind.

"I hope one day you'll change your mind, but that wasn't what I wanted to say. I only hope that after we have this conversation, you'll still be willing to allow me to court you, never mind actually ask you to be my wife."

She tilted her head to the side as though trying to make sense of his words.

He took a deep breath and continued. "I need to tell you the truth about what happened the day your husband died. It wasn't a hunting accident, as Brantford told you. Laughton died after fighting a duel."

She didn't seem surprised. It was just the sort of foolish behavior in which her husband had often engaged. "I should have realized as much. Given how many men he'd cuckolded during the ten years of our marriage, I suppose it was inevitable. I'm not sure why Lucien kept the information from me, however. He knows I didn't care that Laughton turned his attention elsewhere." She shook her head. "Never mind that now. So, tell me, who do I have to thank for freeing me?"

Ellen was putting up a good front, but Castlefield could see that his words had unsettled her. He'd lay odds, however, that she was more upset by the fact her brother hadn't been honest with her than the discovery her husband hadn't died in a hunting accident.

"Me," he said, meeting her incredulous gaze head-on.

CHAPTER 23

OR SEVERAL SECONDS time itself seemed to stop. She couldn't have heard him correctly. Why would Charles have fought a duel with her husband?

But all too soon, thoughts and emotions bombarded her, and she struggled under their weight. Ellen rose to her feet and turned away, desperately needing a moment to sort through her feelings. She heard Charles stand, but he waited without a word. The silence threatened to suffocate her.

Above everything was her desire to flee. Instead, she turned to face the man who had so casually upended her world. First by introducing her to feelings she'd long thought out of her reach, then by throwing it all away with one word.

He stood tall and silent, waiting for her to speak. The emotion in his dark eyes spoke of his own conflicted feelings. He was so handsome, so dear to her, and a part of her longed to throw herself into his arms. But she refused to give in to that impulse. She'd been so careless with her emotions, and only now, when she realized she might love this man, had she discovered he'd lied to her. Just like her husband had done when he'd courted her.

"I need to go," she said. "I need time to think."

He gave his head a sharp shake. "Stay, Ellen. We have to talk about this."

Sadness. Yes, that's what she was feeling, along with a healthy dose of disbelief that she'd allowed another man to use her emotions against her. Angry at herself for her weakness, she could only lash out at him. "The time to discuss the fact you fought a duel with my husband—one which led to his death— would have been before we became intimate. Tell me, was this all just a game to you?"

She had to give him his due. If she didn't know better, she'd think what she saw reflected in his eyes was grief.

"We both know if I'd told you about the duel before I had the chance to prove I'm nothing like Laughton, you never would have given me that opportunity."

She could only shake her head, incredulous. "You are exactly like my husband."

Charles flinched at the accusation, but she was too angry to stop. A small inner voice urged her to exercise caution, that she shouldn't be lashing out before she'd taken the time to think through the entire situation. She ignored that voice. Charles wanted to talk about this now, and so she'd tell him exactly what she was thinking.

"Like you, Laughton wooed me with sweet words and sweet kisses. But the entire time he was lying about who he really was and what marriage to him would be like. How is what you've done any different? If you could keep this from me, what else will you keep from me?"

"You must know that I care for you. I want honesty between us, which is why I'm telling you this now. You can still walk away, but I'm hoping with every fiber of my being that you don't because what we have is something that most people never find."

She wanted to believe him, but experience had taught her that a man's actions spoke far more about his intentions than mere words ever could. She couldn't understand why her brother had kept this a secret from her. Given everything she'd told him about her marriage, he would have known she didn't care how Laughton had died. He must have hidden the details because Castlefield didn't want anyone to know about his involvement.

"Tell me, would you have told me the truth if my brother weren't here? Did he keep this from me because you asked him to? Is he forcing you to tell me the truth now when you should have done so from the beginning?"

Castlefield shook his head. "Brantford isn't forcing me to do anything."

There was something about his air that told her he still held something back. She crossed her arms and waited for him to continue.

Castlefield blew out of harsh breath. "If you must know, we did talk about this matter and how I needed to tell you the truth. But no, he didn't force my hand. I'm telling you what I told him—I always intended to tell you about the role I played in your husband's death."

"And you thought the appropriate time was after we'd become intimate."

She didn't miss the way his hands clenched as he spoke. "You hated me, Ellen, because of the distance I'd stupidly put between us when we were younger. You wanted nothing to do with me. Is it so foolish that I wanted to remind you of our friendship? To show you that I've regretted pushing you away every day for the past twelve years? The very last thing I wanted when you'd finally consented to spend time with me was to tell you I'd fought a duel with your husband and that he'd died at my hands."

She didn't even try to keep her voice down. "I would have given you a damn medal. I was content to live a life alone, putting in the occasional appearance with Laughton to save face. All I wanted was for him to leave me alone, and I had that. But when he died..." She took a deep breath to steady her voice. "Heaven help me, but I rejoiced when I learned he'd died in a hunting accident. I would have *thanked* you for freeing me from that man."

He looked down. He only seemed to notice then that his fists were clenched, but he didn't—or couldn't —relax them before raising his head to meet her gaze again. "Would you have felt the same way when you realized I couldn't tell you why we'd fought the duel?"

Dread. Yes, that was the emotion she was feeling above any other. She didn't want to have this conversation with Charles because she didn't want to know the truth. The real reason he'd fought that duel.

"You fought over a woman."

He didn't reply, but the way his mouth twisted into a slight grimace told her everything. Was she forever doomed to give her heart to men who were destined to break it? For one thing had become abundantly clear to her: despite her attempts to shield herself from hurt, the man standing before her now had her heart.

He took a step closer but stopped when she took a corresponding one back. "I'm not going to hurt you, damn it, nor am I going to force myself on you."

"Given my previous experience with men who are content to lie to me, you'll have to excuse me if my instinct to protect myself takes over."

His jaw tensed and a brief flash of guilt hit her

before she pushed it aside. She could almost see him mentally sifting through what he wanted to say to her.

They stood facing each other for several long moments. Her eyes darted down to his hands again, which had opened and closed, and she realized he was trying to keep himself from reaching out for her.

Unable to bear the silence, she spoke first. "Why didn't you tell me the truth? I know you didn't live the life of a monk." She couldn't help the bitter laugh that escaped. "If I was under any illusions before, your prowess in the bedroom proved otherwise."

"Ellen—"

The sound of her name on his lips, the emotion behind it tortured, reminded her too much of the nights they'd spent together. "Do you regret lying to me?"

Resignation settled in his expression. "I won't lie to you again. Given the same circumstances, and knowing what I do now, I wouldn't change a thing."

She'd expected him to prevaricate, and so it took her a moment to find her voice. "And what circumstances are those?"

"All of it. I'd approach you the same way and I wouldn't change one thing that happened between us. I knew we'd be good together, but to make you see it —" One corner of his mouth lifted in a smile, but the emotion behind it was filled with sadness. "No, you never would have given me a second chance if you'd known the truth first. I acted in the only manner possible."

She couldn't believe that after everything, he'd cling to his insistence that it had been necessary to lie to her. A coldness began to seep through her, one that she welcomed. It was the same coldness that had allowed her to survive Laughton's angry words long after he'd stopped touching her.

"Knowing how much I value honesty, will you tell me whom you and my husband fought over?"

He took a long time to reply, much longer than was necessary if he was going to answer her question. Castlefield professed to care for her, and a large part of her was inclined to believe he was being truthful. But they would never have a future together if he insisted on keeping secrets from her.

"Ask me anything else," he said when he finally replied.

The pleading note in his voice would have swayed her before today, but she was now almost completely dead inside. Again.

She already knew the answer to the question, but she asked it anyway. "Did you kill him for me?"

He seemed at a loss as to how to proceed. Finally he said, "I didn't know. Your brother kept your secrets well."

"But you did kill him because of another woman."

His silence spoke volumes.

"I see." She had to take a deep breath before dipping into a brief curtsy. "Thank you for your hospitality, but I fear I have imposed too long. I regret that I'll have to decline Jane's invitation to join her family in Brighton, but I'll be sure to make it up to her the next time we're both in town."

"Don't go." Castlefield's voice broke on the words. If she were still capable of feeling, her heart would have done the same.

"I would appreciate it if you didn't tell anyone yet about my decision to return home. I'll leave a note for Rose and my brother. There's no reason my departure should interfere with their stay. If you could arrange for a coach to be brought around, I'll wait for it in my room. A maid can pack my things later and they can be returned at your convenience."

"I love you, Ellen. I'd thought allowing you to marry Laughton was the biggest mistake of my life. I was wrong—this is. Failing to make you see just how much I care for you. How much I love you. Knowing what you've already been through with the first man who professed to love you, I won't force my attentions on you."

Ellen looked away as he spoke. She'd thought she was dead inside, but hearing him say that he loved her had brought her traitorous heart back to life. It was a good thing she no longer allowed that organ to rule her actions.

"I want you to know, however, that I'll be waiting

for you. I can only pray you'll realize that what we have is special. That I'm not the same man your husband was."

Somehow Ellen made herself meet his gaze. It took a supreme amount of strength not to crumble at the mixture of devastation and determination she saw written on the face of the man she loved.

She couldn't manage any words, and she didn't think her legs would hold long enough to allow her to give him another curtsy. Instead, she inclined her head and moved past him, refusing to hurry as she left the garden.

One thing was certain as the scents of the garden enveloped her during her walk back to the house. She'd never again be able to smell another rose without having it call to mind her current heartbreak.

She half hoped Castlefield would stop her again, but he kept his word and allowed her to go.

She managed to make it to her bedroom before she allowed the tears to flow.

CHAPTER 24

*E*LLEN PERMITTED HERSELF the brief respite of her emotions before going about the arduous process of pulling herself together again. It would be easier once she returned to London and could immerse herself in her former life. Brantford had also withheld the truth from her, but she'd get over that betrayal before long.

Rose would be disappointed when she discovered Ellen had gone, as would Jane when she learned Ellen wouldn't be visiting Brighton. Ellen could only hope their rekindled friendship would survive her disappointment.

As she waited for news that the carriage had been readied, her gaze went to the wooden box that rested on her dressing table. Her brief relationship with Charles was over, yet she couldn't find it in her heart to spurn his gift. She no longer believed the conch shell it contained would bring her luck, yet she couldn't leave it behind. Even if it only served as a reminder not to let down her guard with another man, she needed to take it with her.

It took every ounce of strength she possessed not to break down again when her gaze drifted to the bed and memories assailed her of the night they'd spent together.

She sat at her dressing table and placed the box on her lap. With one finger she traced the shells etched along the lid as she waited. She needed to write a quick note to Castlefield's mother to thank her for her hospitality. And Rose would be disappointed to discover she'd left without so much as a goodbye. She closed her eyes and took another deep breath to steady her nerves.

Before she could reach for the quill and paper that were in a drawer of the dressing table, a knock sounded at the door. Expecting a maid or a footman, she stood and called out for the person to enter. But when the door opened, it was her brother who strode into the room.

He closed the door quietly and turned to face her. "You're leaving."

It wasn't a question, and he didn't appear surprised.

"Did it ever occur to you that I should have been told my husband died as a result of a duel?"

Brantford raised a brow, and she had to hold back

the urge to yell at him. How could he have allowed her to grow close to Castlefield when he knew it would only end in heartbreak? She wrapped her arms around her waist, not caring that he'd recognize the action for what it was—an attempt to hold herself together.

"Don't play games with me. The only reason you'd be here was if Charles told you about our talk." He said nothing, and a horrible realization struck her. "You were there. He didn't give me any details, but we both know there's only one person he would have asked to be his second. And you had the connections to cover it up afterward."

"What would you have me say, Ellen? Of course I knew. And no, I won't apologize."

Ellen gave her head a small shake. "Of course not. Why would you, the man who manipulates everyone around him, ever apologize for having a hand in my husband's death?"

His impassive facade cracked just a bit at her accusation. "Laughton's death was a blessing. Don't pretend you cared for him."

She wouldn't go down that thorny path with him. Not when they both knew he was speaking the truth. "The point is you lied to me about it."

"We lied to everyone. Did you really want to be the subject of all the gossip that would have surrounded the two of you? You'd made your dislike for Castlefield known. The last thing you would have wanted was for the two of you to become linked in the ensuing scandal. Castlefield's name and position in society would have provided him with a measure of immunity, but the old hens would have ripped your reputation to shreds."

"Gossip? That's your excuse for hiding the truth from me?" She gave a dry, bitter laugh. "What are a few words when I've suffered far worse? But I never thought you would lie to me. And Charles..." Her voice broke, and she had to take a deep breath before continuing. "Castlefield is no better than my husband. He wouldn't confirm the reason for the duel, but if it involved Laughton, we both know it was over some woman's honor."

And there it was, the real reason for her anger. Charles and Laughton had dueled over another woman. Despite the fact she and Charles had known one another since they were children and he claimed he'd developed deeper feelings for her before she wed another man, he hadn't come to her rescue. It didn't matter that he hadn't known what she suffered during those early years of her marriage before Brantford had stepped in and taught her how to defend herself. Her heart cared nothing for logic.

Brantford frowned. "There's more to it than that."

"Then tell me, because heaven knows he won't."

She hated the way her voice hid nothing of her hurt. Even worse, her formerly emotionless brother's brows drew together in sadness.

"I can't. But please don't leave. Not like this." When she didn't reply, he added, "What of Jane? She's expecting you in Brighton."

Ellen looked away, fighting the tears that threatened to spill again. "I can't stay under this roof a moment longer, and more than anything, I need to be alone right now. My friendship with Jane will survive this—I'll make sure of it. But I can't stay here."

Brantford closed the distance between them and placed a hand on her arm. "Ellen…"

She angrily wiped away an errant tear that threatened to spill. There would be time enough for crying later when she was alone in the carriage.

"I can't stay here, Lucien. I can't see him again. You taught me how to defend myself against my husband's fists, but how can I defend myself against Charles's honeyed words? Knowing he would never raise a hand to me in anger will be small comfort when he takes another lover."

When her brother didn't reply, she turned to face him. Only when her eyes met his did he speak. "He cares about you. He always has."

"If he cares so much, he never should have kept this from me." *And he never should have allowed me to suffer at the hands of my husband when he had no qualms about fighting a duel with the man over the honor of another woman.*

She was acting irrationally, she knew that, but she had to get away. There were too many people here. And how could she face Charles's mother or Rose?

Both wanted nothing more than to see Ellen wed to the man, and Ellen, fool that she was, had actually considered making that possibility a reality.

No, she needed to get away, spend some time alone so she could mourn the end of this dream. Fairy-tale endings were something that happened to other women. She'd pulled herself together once before when she realized that her husband didn't love her, and she would do it again now. It would be much harder this time, but she vowed silently that she *would* move past this.

$\mathcal{N}$UMBNESS HAD SETTLED over her, finally, when she arrived at her brother's town house in London. It was early afternoon, too early to retire, yet she left instructions with the staff that she wasn't to be disturbed and made her way to her bedroom.

She'd spent most of the four-hour trip struggling to push back the emotions that warred within her. Anger, betrayal... but chief among them was embarrassment. Once again she'd allowed herself to be played the fool by a man. Only this time was much worse. She realized now that what she'd once thought was love when she'd married Laughton had been youthful infatuation.

No, there was only one man she loved, one man she'd ever loved. And like her husband, he refused to be honest with her.

The rest of the day dragged, and it was with relief that she crawled between the sheets of her bed that evening. But instead of finding refuge in sleep, she tossed and turned all night. The sun was beginning to rise when exhaustion finally won and she slipped into an uneasy slumber.

It was almost midday when her maid roused her with news that she had a guest.

Expecting that her brother had followed her, she didn't hold back her huff of annoyance as she cast off her blankets and settled onto the edge of the bed. She wasn't successful in her attempt not to glare at the hapless woman.

"I told you I wasn't to be disturbed. If my brother wishes to speak to me, he can wait until later."

"It isn't Lord Brantford," the woman said, moving to the wardrobe to fetch a day dress.

Ellen's heart began to race as she struggled with the thought that Charles might have followed her. But no, he'd said he'd wait for her to take the next step. The game was over and they'd both lost. He wouldn't have followed her all the way to London when he'd let her go so easily in the first place.

"Who is it," she asked, moving to the dressing table while the maid took her place behind Ellen and began combing out her hair.

"Lady Eddings," she said. "She's waiting for you in the drawing room."

Ellen closed her eyes at the news and struggled

with her disappointment. While she was relieved there would be no more messy arguments with Charles—no, she must think of him as Castlefield now—she still wanted to maintain her friendship with Jane. And clearly her friend hadn't been happy to discover Ellen wouldn't be visiting her in Brighton after all.

Determined not to allow her rift with Castlefield to impact her relationship with Jane, Ellen sat still while her maid finished pinning up her hair before helping her into the pale yellow dress she'd selected.

Ellen had expected to have more time to come to terms with everything that had happened, but it was clear she'd have no reprieve from the affair today.

A quarter of an hour after her maid had woken her, she crossed the threshold into the drawing room. Jane rose swiftly from her seat on the settee. Her expression was clear, but Ellen had seen the frown on her friend's face when she first entered the room.

Jane drew her into a quick hug before stepping back to examine her face. Ellen knew what she'd see—eyes that were still puffy from the many tears she'd shed in the carriage the previous day. She must have looked worse than she thought, however, for Jane took her by the hand and led her to the settee, drawing her down next to her.

"I'm so sorry," Jane said. "This is all my fault."

Ellen frowned, surprised Jane would feel the need to apologize. "You're not to blame for encouraging a match between your brother and me. But the fact that it will never happen doesn't have to affect our friendship."

Jane clasped her hands in her lap. She'd removed her gloves, and Ellen could see that her knuckles were white with how tightly she'd twined her fingers.

Ellen found it difficult to sit still. She wasn't ready to discuss this with Jane. The hurt was still too new, but she knew the subject couldn't be avoided, so she vowed to get it over with as quickly as possible. Then she could go about setting her life to rights again.

"Did your brother tell you what happened between him and my husband?"

"If you're referring to the duel they fought, then yes, I know about it. I've known from the beginning."

To her credit, Jane didn't look away, but Ellen couldn't hold her gaze. She closed her eyes as a sense of betrayal washed over her. Jane said nothing, waiting for her to process the information.

"So everyone knew but me?"

Unable to sit still any longer, she rose and crossed the room to look through the front window. Jane's carriage waited outside, and a shadowy figure could be seen through the carriage window. It must be Lord Eddings. He wouldn't have wanted his wife to make the trip into town alone. She wondered if he, too, knew about the duel.

"Ellen—"

"It doesn't bother me that he killed my husband. Heaven knows the day I was freed from my marriage to that man was the happiest day of my life. I'm not proud to admit that, but it's true nonetheless."

She turned to face Jane again. "Do you know they fought over a woman? As if it isn't bad enough that my husband had affairs with heaven only knows how many women, but now I've discovered that Charles —" Her voice actually cracked. Giving her head a sharp shake, she took a deep breath and continued. "Now I know Castlefield is the same. That knowledge shouldn't bother me, but it does."

"It wasn't like that—"

Ellen cut off Jane's attempt to excuse her brother's behavior. "Of course it was. And to make matters worse, I allowed myself to be taken in by his charm and his lies. Again. When will I ever learn that men can't be trusted?" She turned away and looked out the window again. "I was beginning to allow myself to believe Castlefield cared for me. That perhaps he might even come to love me. But it was all just a game. Another way to get back at Laughton for whatever rivalry they had. And I know they were rivals. Castlefield made no qualms about hiding how much he hated my husband when he first learned of our betrothal."

Ellen tried to hold on to her anger, but as the full realization of her error in judgment settled over her, that anger seeped away to be replaced by a bone-deep shame. She returned to the settee and sank onto it, then dropped her head into her hands. "I'm such a fool to have fallen for his lies. Why do I keep allowing myself to be taken in by men?"

"They fought the duel over me."

Jane's words were spoken so softly that Ellen almost missed them. She lifted her head and stared at her friend in disbelief. "I know you weren't lying when you told me you didn't have an affair with my husband."

"I didn't." Jane took a deep breath before continuing. "Laughton approached me about having an affair and I declined. But what I never told you was that he tried to force himself on me while I was pregnant with Hope. I struggled and fell to the ground."

There was silence for almost a full minute as Ellen stared at Jane in disbelief. She was still trying to think of what to say when Jane continued. "He only stopped when he saw the blood and I told him I was with child."

Horror swept through her, and she closed her eyes briefly, finally connecting the reason behind her friend's precarious pregnancy. And why Jane hadn't wanted to see her for the past two years. "I'm so sorry. I didn't know," she finally managed, knowing the words weren't enough. "Is that why you didn't want to see me?" She looked away, her shoulders sagging. "Of course it was. If I hadn't kept Laughton at a distance, none of this would have happened. How many other women suffered his attentions just so I could remain safe?"

"Of course not." Jane reached out and placed a hand over Ellen's. "I never blamed you for your husband's actions."

Ellen knew that Jane was speaking the truth. If their situations had been reversed, she certainly wouldn't have blamed Jane. But it was difficult not to feel responsible. "Why didn't you tell me?"

"I didn't want to tell anyone. Not even my husband knows. I was too afraid of what he would do, and that he'd end up getting himself killed. But my brother found me after it happened, and it was he who called for the doctor. I couldn't keep the truth from him when I realized he'd seen Laughton leave the room. But you should know Laughton didn't touch me intimately. He never got that chance."

"But he did push you."

"I don't really know what happened. I was struggling to get away from him at the time. It's possible he simply released me and, in my attempt to draw away from him, I overbalanced and fell backward."

Ellen didn't contradict her friend, but she knew her husband. When Jane had resisted him, he would have had no qualms about throwing her to the ground. If he hadn't panicked at the sight of the blood his actions had caused... She sent up a silent prayer of thanks that everything had turned out well in the end. Neither Jane nor the baby she'd been carrying at the time had been hurt.

"So your brother fought the duel instead of your

husband. And my brother helped him so everyone would think it was a hunting accident."

"Yes," Jane said. "I tried to stop Charles from issuing the challenge, to convince him that nothing had actually happened. That Laughton hadn't violated me. But he was filled with rage and wouldn't be persuaded otherwise."

Ellen could only shake her head in disbelief. "Why didn't he tell me? When I accused him of dueling with Laughton over the affections of another woman, he didn't deny it. He could easily have told me what had happened."

Jane's grip on her hand became stronger. "I made him promise he would never reveal what had happened. I don't think he even told your brother when he elicited his assistance as his second. Brantford must have guessed and helped in setting up the fiction about the accident. It's the only reason my husband has never learned about what really happened that day. My brother is a good man. He kept that promise, even when it meant losing you."

"Laughton almost ruined all of us. He certainly took away any delusions I'd had of living happily ever after with any man. I only thank the heavens that he didn't cause you to lose your daughter."

"No, he hasn't ruined any of us and certainly not you. You still have that chance of a future together with someone who cares about you a great deal."

Ellen withdrew her hand from her friend's grasp

and looked away. "I was so cold and distant to him before I left. I have no doubt he's realized his life would be far easier if he found a wife who was more agreeable than me."

"I'm sure that's true," Jane said with a slight smile, "but he doesn't want anyone else. He's been trying to forget you since you married Laughton. I didn't realize it at first since I'm several years younger than the two of you, but he loves you and has done so for years."

Ellen stared at Jane, unable to hold back the thread of hope that was blossoming within her. But beyond that, she didn't want to. Her friend was correct. Laughton hadn't ruined everything, but that would only be true if she didn't allow his specter to continue hanging over her. She'd allowed his memory, and that of their unhappy marriage, to cloud everything she'd done.

But she'd seen with her own eyes that not all men were as controlling as her deceased husband. That happiness was possible between a man and a woman. Jane was in one such union. Even her brother, who many believed to have ice water running through his veins, was capable of love. And one thing was undeniable. Lucien had seen true evil. He'd never supported her betrothal to Laughton, had never thought the man good enough for her, but she'd dismissed his reservations, ascribing them to the beliefs of an over-protective sibling. It wasn't until after she was married that she realized her brother had seen something in Laughton that she, and everyone else, had missed.

But Lucien had no such reservations about Castle-field. If there was one certainty in this world, it was that her brother was a good judge of character. If he approved of his friend's intention to marry her, that was as good a recommendation as one could get.

"Where is he, Jane? I have to go to him."

Jane smiled and wrapped her friend in a tight embrace before pulling back. "It's about time."

CHAPTER 26

*I*T TOOK ELLEN a few minutes to sift through her options and decide what she needed to do.

She considered going to Charles and apologizing for... everything, really. For doubting him, for attempting to keep her emotions locked away even while he was open and honest with her. But most of all for not trusting him. They both knew her behavior was directly linked to her history with Laughton, but she wanted to make it up to him. A simple apology wouldn't be enough. That meant she needed to perform a grand gesture.

Determination filled her as she issued instructions to the staff and went up to her bedroom to collect the one thing she needed for the trip—the box that contained the conch shell she and Charles had found together when they were children.

She was in the carriage with Jane and Lord Eddings and on their way back to Sussex before Ellen could fully take in just how quickly her life had changed. She was acting impulsively, something which she tried never to do, but every fiber of her being told her she was doing the right thing. The time for doubt had long since passed.

The journey was a quiet one. She smiled fondly as Lord Eddings wrapped an arm around his wife and drew her to his side, where Jane rested her head on his shoulder. Ellen wanted so much the ability to be that free with Castlefield; it was an ache that threatened to steal her breath.

She wanted to continue the previous conversation, but she could say nothing lest she betray Jane's secret to Lord Eddings. It had taken a great deal of courage on her friend's part to share the truth with her, but Ellen couldn't shake her belief that what had happened was partially her fault. There was no doubt in her mind Laughton had been striking out at Ellen in an act of revenge when he'd attempted to force himself on Jane.

When they reached Castlefield's estate it was early evening. Ellen gave the other woman a tight hug, thanking her for coming to fetch her and promising to visit them in Brighton. Before stepping out of the carriage, she lowered her voice and whispered, "Tell him" into Jane's ear. When she pulled back, Jane gave her a firm nod and Ellen felt her heart swell in relief. The time for secrets was over.

A footman had opened the carriage door, and Ellen thanked the couple one more time before bidding them adieu for now.

Eddings reached for his wife's hand and said, "I'm glad you changed your mind. Castlefield is a good man, and I would see him as happy as we are."

Ellen could only nod in reply, a lump forming in her throat as she allowed the footman to help her down from the carriage. She spared a moment to wave at Jane and Lord Eddings one final time as the carriage pulled away to whisk the occupants back to their new home in Brighton.

The footman bowed and offered to take the box Ellen was still clutching. She declined, telling him she needed to keep it with her for now.

She didn't hesitate before asking the question that was uppermost in her mind. "Do you know where His Grace is at the moment?"

"He's been in his study all day."

Ellen thanked the young man and made her way into the house. She hadn't even gotten past the drawing room before a voice called out to her. She wasn't surprised to find her brother seated in a wing chair, fingers steepled on his chest, waiting for her.

Sighing, she entered the room. Now that she'd made up her mind to take a wild leap of faith, she didn't want to delay another second.

Brantford got right to the point. "I'm not going to ask for details, but I wanted to say how glad I am you've returned."

It struck her then that her brother had been responsible for this morning's events. "You told Jane I'd returned to London."

He inclined his head and rose to his feet. "Someone had to mend the mess you and Castlefield had managed to make of things."

She hugged him by way of response. He allowed the moment to continue longer than he would have before he'd found love himself. That was yet another thing for which she needed to thank Rose. Her brother of old would have made a cutting comment when she released him, but now Brantford merely gave her an indulgent smile when she stepped back.

"He's left word with the staff that he's not to be disturbed, but I believe he'll make an exception in your case."

Ellen managed a firm nod before making her way to the study. Butterflies rioted in her belly, but she forced herself to ignore them, concentrating solely on the task at hand—letting Charles know that she trusted him and that she wanted a future together. When she'd left, he'd told her he would wait for her. Only a day had passed, but it was entirely possible he'd decided in the hours since they'd spoken that waiting for her was more trouble than it was worth.

Heaven knew he'd expended an infinite amount of patience on her already.

Her knock was met by a surly response to go away. She took a deep breath and opened the door.

"Goddamn it—" His outburst cut off when he saw her.

Outside the bedroom, she couldn't recall ever seeing him so disheveled. He hadn't bothered to shave that morning, dark stubble colored his jawline, and his hair bore signs that he'd run his fingers through the dark locks several times.

Her heart twisted at the visible signs of how much she'd hurt this man. "I know you asked not to be disturbed, but I was hoping that didn't apply to me."

He stood and moved around the desk to stand before her. When his gaze fell on the box in her hand, his jaw clenched and he looked away. "If you're here to return my gift, you needn't have gone to the trouble."

Ellen hated the note of defeat in his voice. Did he really think so little of her as to believe she'd returned to Sussex just to throw his gift back in his face? A pang of remorse struck her as she realized she'd behaved so shabbily toward him that she shouldn't be surprised at his assumption.

She set the box down on his desk and lifted the lid. She could feel the weight of his gaze on her as she removed the conch and held it out to him. "I'm here to tell you that I've made a wish."

When he didn't reach for the shell, she took a deep breath and lowered herself to rest on one knee. The expression on his face would have been amusing if fear that she was too late wasn't threatening to steal her breath.

His jaw loosened and his mouth opened before he got control of himself and closed it again. "What are you playing at, Ellen?"

"Actually, I'm taking a gamble that I haven't ruined everything between us. I've decided that the one thing I want most in this world is a future with you. If you'll have me, of course." He seemed dumbstruck by her words, so she continued. "I am asking you, Your Grace, if you would consent to becoming my husband. I recognize that it might take some time for you to decide whether you want to take such a risk with me—"

He took the shell with one hand and with the other he pulled her to her feet. After placing her peace offering back in the box that rested on his desk, he pulled her into his arms. His embrace threatened to crush her, but she didn't care. She was exactly where she wanted to be.

He pulled back and frowned down at her. "You scared the hell out of me. I thought losing you once was bad, but twice was almost more than I could bear."

"Jane came to see me, and she told me every-thing." Ellen waited a moment, not sure what she

222

expected from the man before her, but it wasn't silence. "You should be angry with me," she said finally when he didn't speak.

His brows drew together. "Why?"

"Because I didn't believe you. Because I jumped to the worst conclusions about you when all you were doing was protecting Jane and keeping your promise to her."

He shook his head before tilting it to the side. "How could I blame you after everything you've been through? Of course I'm not angry with you. I love you. I'm only grateful you're willing to give me another chance to prove what I've come to know… that we are made for one another."

Ellen raised a hand and placed it along his cheek. The rasp of whiskers tickled the skin of her palm. "I've always loved you, Charles. It just took me far longer than it should have to realize it. I loved you first as a friend and now as a man. I'm not sure anyone else in this world could have tempted me to risk my heart again."

There were no more words after that as he lowered his head to claim her mouth and her soul.

EPILOGUE

August 1808
On the road to Brighton

IT WAS ONLY MIDDAY, but his wife was already exhausted. Unable to hold out against the lulling sway of the well-sprung carriage, Ellen nestled against his shoulder and closed her eyes.

Castlefield chuckled as he shifted slightly to allow Ellen to rest more comfortably against him.

She tilted her head to one side and gave him a mock glare. "Don't you dare laugh at me. It's your fault I'm in this state."

He placed a possessive hand against the slight swell of her midsection. "I didn't hear you complaining when we spent all that time trying to conceive."

She sighed. "I'm not even four months along. How am I going to last another five months?"

It took only a minute for Ellen's breathing to deepen, signaling she'd slipped into sleep. He kissed the top of her head before laying his head against the plush seat cushions, reveling in the feel of his wife lying in his arms. The light scent she wore wrapped around him.

He didn't realize he'd also drifted into sleep until the carriage jerked to a stop and woke him.

"I wondered when you'd wake up," Ellen said, straightening from where she still rested against him.

She arched a brow in challenge, but he didn't rise to the bait. They both knew Ellen had just woken as well.

When she lifted a hand to pat at her hair, he shook his head. "You look beautiful, as always."

Ellen laughed. "You've already won me. You needn't continue to flatter me."

"It's not flattery if it's true."

Her eyes softened and a fond smile spread across her lips. "And to think I almost let you go."

"We both know you're too smart to have let that happen. But you did have me worried for a bit."

The carriage door opened, and he stepped down first before turning to help his wife. Not that she needed his assistance since she still practiced the moves her brother had taught her for her own defense every day. And heaven knew she was still capable of tossing him to the ground. When he grumbled about it, she told him she was doing her part to keep him sharp. But the truth was he didn't mind, especially since she normally followed him down and rewarded his patience with her.

Ellen took his arm and together they made their way to his sister's spacious summer home in Brighton. Fond memories assailed him. Just one short year before, his entire life had changed and he and Ellen had spent an enjoyable month together here after announcing their betrothal. Now they had another announcement.

The door opened just as they reached it, and his sister's family spilled out to welcome them. Eddings smiled fondly at his son as Henry executed a formal bow in greeting. Castlefield swept the boy into his arms, taking delight in Henry's squeals of joy as he dangled him upside down for several seconds.

Not to be left out, Hope lifted her arms to him, saying simply, "Up."

He returned his nephew to his feet, taking a moment to ruffle his hair for good measure, before obliging his niece. A squeal caught his attention, and he turned to see Jane had thrown her arms around Ellen.

"I'm so happy for you," Jane said, stepping back.

He wasn't even embarrassed by the besotted grin that spread across his face when Ellen's gaze met his, joy shining in her expression.

~

Thank you for reading *The Unsuitable Duke.* If you enjoyed this book, you can share that enjoyment by recommending it to others and leaving a review.

To learn when Suzanna has a new release, you can sign up to receive an email alert at:
https://www.suzannamedeiros.com/newsletter/

To read more about the author's books and learn where you can buy copies, you can visit the "Books" page on the author's website:
https://www.suzannamedeiros.com/books/

ABOUT THE AUTHOR

USA Today bestselling author Suzanna Medeiros was born and raised in Toronto, Canada. Her love for the written word led her to pursue a degree in English Literature from the University of Toronto. She went on to earn a Bachelor of Education degree, but graduated at a time when no teaching jobs were available. After working at a number of interesting places, including a federal inquiry, a youth probation office, and the Office of the Fire Marshal of Ontario, she decided to pursue her first love—writing.

Suzanna is married to her own hero and is the proud mother of twin daughters. She is an avowed romantic who enjoys spending her days writing love stories.

She would like to thank her parents for showing her that love at first sight and happily ever after really do exist.

To learn more about Suzanna's books, you can visit her website at:
https://www.suzannamedeiros.com

or visit her on Facebook at:
https://www.facebook.com/AuthorSuzannaMedeiros

To learn when she has a new release available, you can sign up for her new release mailing list at:
https://www.suzannamedeiros.com/newsletter

BOOKS BY SUZANNA MEDEIROS

Dear Stranger

Forbidden in February (A Year Without a Duke)

The Novellas: A Collection

Landing a Lord series:

Dancing with the Duke

Loving the Marquess

Beguiling the Earl

The Unaffected Earl

The Unsuitable Duke

The Unexpected Marquess — Coming Soon

Hathaway Heirs series:

Lady Hathaway's Indecent Proposal

Lord Hathaway's New Bride

The Captain's Heart

Miss Hathaway's Wish — Coming Soon

For more information please visit the "Books" page on the author's website:

https://www.suzannamedeiros.com/books/